# FIRE IN THE BLOOD

GRAEME DONNELLY

# COPYRIGHT

# Contents

# Chapter One

*San Francisco, California*
*Present day…*

Finn Mason stood at the back door of the restaurant and breathed in the cool San Francisco air. In less than an hour, his first restaurant, *Homefires*, would open to the public and he could barely believe it. *From Kansas to this*. He shook his head. Yes, so many things could go wrong—no-one could turn up to eat in the small place in the Castro District with its casual atmosphere and refined cuisine. The food was served on trays which the customer would eat while settled on large, comfortable sofas—tv dinners with a fine dining twist.

It was a risk, absolutely, but Finn was going with his gut and playing on the whole Netflix-and-chill vibe that had taken over from clubbing and partying of late.

He felt Aiden's arms slip around his waist and his lips against the back of his neck. "Hey, you."

"Hey, big guy."

"Jitters?"

"A little."

Finn turned in his arms, grinning. Aiden's brown eyes crinkled at the edges as he smiled. Finn traced the fine crow's feet with the tip of his finger. Aiden Fox was well named for his appearance. His dark blonde hair, scattered with grey, stuck up around the edges of his chef's hat and his sharply-angled face looked younger than his forty-two years. Finn cupped his lover's cheek in his hand. "It's okay to be nervous, right?"

"You'd be insane not to be. You did it, buddy. You made this place a reality."

"*We* did it," Finn insisted, but he was buoyed by Aiden's words.

Thirteen months ago, this place had been a burned-out shell, a red-brick hole-in-the-wall club on the corner of one of the less popular streets in the district. The realtor had warned them against the property, even though he himself had tried to dump it from his portfolio as fast as he could. "This place has had its share of crappy luck," he told them. "The fire, then there are all kinds of rumors of murders and beatings and god knows what else kind of shit goes on in these places."

"*These* places?" Finn had lifted an eyebrow, and the realtor held up his hands.

"Hey, I mean clubs in general, not just gay clubs, man. Don't take offense."

Finn and Aiden had shared a loaded glance, but Finn decided to let it go. There was something about the place… he didn't know if it was because of the way it felt unloved, misunderstood or the way it had just been left to rot. It felt like it was an underdog. Or, he thought with a grin, it could just have been because of the *spectacular* views over the Bay that the upstairs rooms had afforded.

Aiden left the decision entirely up to him. "Babe, you're the creative force behind this whole thing. If it feels right, I trust you."

"But what do *you* think?"

Aiden grinned. "Listen, I'm a burned-out wreck too. I love this place."

And that had been the moment Finn knew this was right. Thanks to Aiden's father, Glenn, loaning them the money, they had gotten the place for a steal, but renovating and fitting the kitchen to Finn's exact specifications had taken forever. Well, thirteen months, Finn grinned to himself now.

He looked at Aiden again, who was watching him carefully. "You ready for this?" Aiden's voice was soft. Finn nodded.

"I'm good. Let's get the *mise en place* finished up."

"All done."

Aiden was Finn's sous chef, unofficially of course, due to his lack of official training, but Finn wouldn't have had anyone else as his right-hand man. Aiden could read his mood, often his mind, when it came to running the kitchen. And what Aiden didn't know about wine wasn't worth knowing. Of course, now, he didn't drink—the court-ordered membership of *Narcotics Anonymous* had forbidden that particular vice.

Aiden disappeared back into the restaurant and Finn followed him, diverting to the restrooms for one last break before service began.

As he splashed his face with water, he studied his reflection, noting with satisfaction that the look in his cornflower-blue eyes was one of determination with only a dash of fear. At thirty-two, Finn Mason bore the scars of so much pain, physical and mental, that he feared the enormity of this day would make him break.

But he *wasn't* breaking. He combed his messy black hair into a semblance of a style, then washed his hands for the third time. *No, stop.* He dried his hands, taking a deep breath, and stepping away from the sink. *Nothing will change if you wash your hands an even amount of times. Nothing good, nothing bad.* The mantra he had been saying in his head for years. *Break the cycle.* His short-lived therapist from back in Kansas had at least helped him out with his OCD, if nothing else. Finn hadn't realized that sometimes therapists could be homophobic assholes too.

Finn went out into the kitchen, smiling gratefully at Aiden, and his other kitchen staff. There was Miko, the petite dessert queen, who took no argument from anybody, especially men twice her size. Jamie, the quiet, reserved English line cook who knew more about flavor than anyone Finn knew, even himself. Berto and Clyde, second sous chef and fry chef respectively, who were in a relationship and were the kitchen's comic relief. And Lisa, the *chef de partie*, indispensable in almost every aspect of kitchen life but so introverted and insular that Finn sometimes wondered if she even knew where she was half the time. Lisa would never join them for the meal Finn would cook for them at the end of every service, muttering her goodbyes after she'd cleaned her station and disappearing before Finn could try to persuade her to stay.

"Well…" Finn had no idea how to make a rousing speech to his troops and he felt his face flame red as he stuttered over a few lines of bland nonsense before stopping. He sighed, hearing Aiden chuckle behind him, and threw up his hands. "Fuck it, this is *it,* dudes. Let's kick some ass."

"Well said." Berto clapped his boss on the back.

Sarah, their hostess at the front of the house, stuck her head around the kitchen door. "Time?"

"Yup. Open up."

Finn didn't know what he had expected to happen right now, but it wasn't this. Maybe he felt it would feel more momentous, that it would either be one thing or the other—complete silence or an influx of curious customers.

Instead, a steady stream of apathetic people drifted in and out, some ordering nothing more than bar snacks. The ticket orders came through sporadically and although the kitchen ran like a dream, it was hardly taxing.

Now Finn was beginning to feel something other than terror. Disappointment. He'd expected either a spectacular success or spectacular failure not this… indifference.

His face must have registered something because at one point, Aiden bore him off outside. "Stop it."

"What?"

"That face. You're being down on yourself. What did you expect? We're new and we have to build up trust."

Finn was silent for a long time. "I just… I don't want to be mediocre."

"And you're *not*, for Christ's sake. People need time to figure out we're here, get word of mouth around. It's not like either us were household names here. They'll get to know us." Aiden's hands fluttered to his pocket and away. Back in the old days, the ever-present pack of cigarettes would be out right now, but like alcohol, Aiden had sworn off them when he kicked the hard stuff. But it was a sign that Aiden wasn't as relaxed as he made out either.

"You think we should have had a bigger opening? Made a statement?"

Aiden shrugged. "Maybe. I mean, it's not like we couldn't have asked my father for money to do that."

"No, we've already asked too much of him." Finn shook his head. Glenn Fox might have bankrolled them this far, but there was no way Finn was allowing more debt to build up. It was a matter of pride as well as anything else.

"We could at least hire a social media guru." Aiden suggested now, leaning against the red brick wall.

"We can't afford one." Finn shrugged. "We'll just have to build a word-of-mouth campaign on our own."

"How?"

Finn grinned at his lover. "By being the best damn restaurant on Castro."

"*Word*, brother. Better get back to it then."

Service picked up after ten p.m. as people came to eat before heading to the clubs. The customers who stayed for more than a drink were initially bemused by the restaurant's casual fixtures and atmosphere then, when they saw the menu, intrigued. Finn's specialty was fine cuisine, but he'd put his own twist on it, making cordon bleu versions of traditional fast foods.

Mac and cheese with shaved truffle, served with a watermelon and arugula salad was the night's best seller, served in mismatched terrines, which added to the rustic, almost-hipster aesthetic of the restaurant. The clientele ate from trays on their laps, sitting on large, comfortable couches set in such a way that they could chat with friends, or meet new people or, if they preferred, enjoy a cozy dinner for two. Finn had even insisted on some single armchairs for any lone customers—he'd spent years eating on his own and knew both sides of that—the bliss of only being with yourself but, on the other hand, the occasional loneliness.

At midnight, the last customers left and, promisingly, they swore to return. Sarah, the hostess came back to the kitchen to tell Finn the restaurant had closed. She wore a bright smile as Finn asked her to gauge the response. "I would say… steady. I think we've made some people ask some questions, and that's a good thing. Don't quote me on this, but I might have had Denny Holt from the *Times* in the restaurant."

Finn paled a little but nodded. "Good. Maybe a review will help."

"Hey, we did okay for a first night without a big opening." Sarah, an experienced hostess in her early forties, patted his arm. "Really, Finn. You did good."

Finn tightened his arms around Aiden as his lover steered the Harley through the midnight streets of San Francisco. It was after one a.m. and the air was much cooler, but Finn enjoyed the sensation of it streaming past his face as Aiden gunned the bike. Their apartment, a way-too-big-for-two-people loft in Oakland, was also thanks to Aiden's family money, but Finn had insisted on paying his half of the mortgage, even if it left him short every month.

Now he gazed out over the bay as they travelled home for the night. San Francisco was a million miles from where he grew up in landlocked Kansas and sometimes, he wondered if all of this was a dream and, in reality, he was still that small-town boy denying who he was and who he loved.

At home, Finn stripped off and stood under the shower, waiting for Aiden to join him. When Aiden was a no-show, Finn cranked off the hot water and went to the bedroom. Aiden was sprawled on his stomach across the bed, snoring gently. Finn grinned to himself. He dried off, dropping the wet towel on the floor and lay down next to his lover. "Move over, you big lug," he whispered, heaving Aiden's big body over to his own side of the bed. Aiden rolled over, grumbling in his sleep, then reached for Finn. Finn went into his arms happily. Nowhere felt quite as safe as in Aiden's big, thickly-muscled arms and Finn let the stress of the day seep from his bones as he gave in to sleep and for once, no nightmares came to ruin his peace.

* * *

Meanwhile, miles away, back in the city, a young man walked calmly along the Golden Gate bridge until he found the right place. Before, months before, he would have laughed at this version of himself, the desperate, hopeless wretch that climbed over the side of the bridge and readied himself to plummet down to oblivion. He would have mocked this man for being so prosaic, so clichéd as to use this place to die, but right now, in the last few moments of his life, he didn't care any more. He had lost. There was nothing left to do. He heard her voice in his head now, telling him how many seconds it took for a body to hit the water, to drop the seventy-five meters to the cold, unforgiving water below.

He didn't waste any more time, pushing away from the steel barrier and tumbling down into the darkness. His last conscious thought was that it turned out she had been right.

It only took four seconds.

# Chapter Two

*New York City*
*Three years ago...*

Finn wished he smoked. He wished he smoked because then he would have an excuse to stay in the alley after he dumped the kitchen trash in the dumpster behind the restaurant. He would have a reason to not go back inside. Marcus was in a stinking mood, had been yelling at everyone in the kitchen all night, and Finn had gotten the worst of it.

He knew it was because of what happened three weeks earlier: Marcus's hand cupping Finn's cock through his jeans. Finn had backed off, actually saying no to his boss. It had been an unexpected come-on and was shocking not just because of Marcus's wife and three kids, but because there had been no hint, no sign at all that Marcus was in any way attracted to him sexually.

Finn had excused himself politely and Marcus hadn't brought it up again, being his usual gruff self with all the staff. Life had gone on as usual—except for tonight. Tonight, there had been a weird energy in the kitchen and Finn was glad, for once, to be the kitchen dogsbody who got to take out the trash.

He leaned back against the cold wall of the restaurant. The alleyway's only light was from a broken lamp, which blinked intermittently, and its piss-yellow illumination matched the ambiance of the Manhattan alley perfectly.

Talk was that Marcus had once been in sniffing distance of a Michelin star, but his cocaine habit had put paid to that dream and now, he ran this midtown... *joint.* That was the most flattering thing Finn could call this place but hell, it was a job, and despite everything, Marcus was a great chef and a useful mentor for someone like him. So, he'd thought before the groping incident. Ever since, he'd come to work with a dread hanging heavy in his chest. Finn had even formulated what he would say to Marcus.

*Sex isn't my thing. I'm pretty much celibate by choice. I like girls. Ha.* Even Finn knew he couldn't get that lie out but the first two were pretty much on the mark. Except they sounded like lame excuses and he went through sleepless nights before he figured out, he could just say no. He'd almost confided in his sister, Hannah, on whose couch he had been sleeping for the last six months, but although she had been the one person in his family to accept his sexuality, she still didn't like to talk about men he might or might not be attracted to.

Not since... *him.*

Finn shook his head now. *Nope. Not going to think about that particular person.* He glanced at his watch, figuring that he'd played hooky for long enough now.

He had pushed open the back door when he heard the shout, the laughter. It was the kind of laughter he knew: mocking, savage. The sound a bully would make.

Finn backed up and checked down towards the commotion. Silhouetted against the end of the alley, he saw a group of people, men, and someone else prone on the floor. They were kicking the shit out of whoever it was. Finn didn't hesitate.

"Hey, motherfuckers!"

The attackers were easily bigger than him, but Finn had learned in his life that confidence and fronting worked miracles in these situations. He stalked towards them, grabbing the first thing his hand came into contact with from the dumpster.

The assailants decided they'd had their fun and left their victim in a pile on the ground as Finn approached. The man lay stricken on the floor, bloodied, and groaning. Finn bent over him.

"Hey, buddy… hey. Are you okay?"

The man rolled onto his back and Finn could see he was either drunk or high, his big brown eyes having difficulty focusing on Finn. His lip was split open and a string of drool dripped down what would obviously be a handsome face, were it not for the shoe prints and bruises on it.

*"Froggle."*

Finn frowned. "What?"

The man wiped ineffectively at his mouth. "Thank you."

Finn reached down and helped him to sit up. The man's torso swayed back and forth and for a moment, Finn thought he might pass out. Instead, the man's eyes focused on what was in Finn's free hand. He started to laugh.

"Dude…" The words still sounded garbled, but this time it was because he was chuckling, "*dude*, did you really rescue me with a baguette in your hand?"

Finn blinked and glanced down. *Yup.* He really had done his whole white knight thing with yesterday's bread. He grinned. "Hey, it worked, didn't it?"

He dumped the bread on the ground and helped the beaten man to his feet. "I'm Finn. Let's get you inside and clean you up. You look like you could use some food and maybe some strong coffee."

He hoisted the man's big arm around his shoulders, feeling the weight of his big frame through his body. "What's your name, buddy?"

The other man grinned at him, and something inside Finn's soul shifted. "Aiden," the man said, "my name is Aiden. Pleased to meet you, Finn."

* * *

*San Francisco,*
*Present day...*

"You're fretting."

"I'm *strategizing*. There's a difference."

Aiden grinned, rolling his eyes. "Whatever you say, babe."

They were sitting in one of their favorite lunchtime places in the city, a Vietnamese place on 4th, and while Aiden was eating his lunch with relish, Finn picked at his, his attention focused more on his notebook. The *blank* page in his notebook. Aiden watched Finn put his pen down with a sigh.

"It's been a month, and we've been steady. I don't want *steady,* I want..." Finn cast around for the right word.

"It's *only* been a month and for a new place, I think we're doing fine."

They'd had this same conversation a million times, but Aiden knew better than to point that out right now. He knew he was right, though. Okay, so, *Homefires* wasn't exactly overflowing with a line of customers out of the door every night, but they had a steady clientele and more importantly, *repeat* clientele. They'd even had some respectable reviews in the local papers.

But, of course, Finn wasn't satisfied. It frustrated Aiden that his love, his sweet Kansas boy, was driven as much by his own lack of self-esteem as he was by his passion for food. Aiden felt it was the thing that held Finn back.

He reached across the table now and took Finn's hand. "Sweets, listen. Every night we fill every table. True, there's no wait list or queue outside… yet. It's been *four* weeks. Strike a balance, babe."

Finn nodded, chewing his bottom lip. "Maybe we should open at lunchtime too."

Aiden sighed and sat back. Finn was in the zone and nothing Aiden could say would snap him out of it. He returned his attention to his food. "What about a social media presence?"

Finn pulled a face and Aiden snickered. "Sometimes I wonder who's the old man here. Finn, you want more, that's an option. Man, some of the dishes you produce are works of art. Imagine putting photos of them on *Instagram* or *Pinterest.*"

Finn grinned then. "You mean, *Pin-interest*?" It was a private joke between them—Finn always, always got it wrong.

"That too." Aiden laughed. "But, seriously, food porn."

"That's a thing?"

"Hell, yes."

Aiden saw a spark of something in Finn's eyes—good. He'd piqued his curiosity.

"The only thing is who would run it? Neither of us have the time."

"Or the knowhow. I'm over forty—I can't be bothered learning new stuff."

Finn grinned. "My old man."

"Yup. Maybe one of the kids knows someone. Miko or Jamie. Even Lisa—she's a nerd."

"How do you know that? Just because she's shy doesn't mean she's a nerd."

Aiden shrugged. "I'll bet you a buffalo nickel she is."

Finn's whole demeanor had brightened. "I still think opening at lunchtime might be a good idea."

"Trial it, then. A couple of days a week. Maybe bar snacks only or something. See who wants to hang out."

Finn smiled at his lover. "You're on."

A week later, Finn was in the kitchen. It was a Saturday, April, and the weather had changed suddenly to bright sunshine. The Castro's hilly streets were buzzing with people and, to Finn's gratification, the lunch sitting at *Homefires* was busy. It was the second time they'd opened early and the success of the first day had only inspired Finn to begin thinking of expanding the menu for the daytime.

Most of his staff had been eager to work longer hours for the extra money, but he'd still had to hire a couple of new staff. One of them, David, was at the bar now as Finn came out to check on orders.

"Couple of sharing platters for that group of four, and the girl at table thirteen asked if we do kale chips. It wasn't on the menu, so I said I'd better check."

Finn shrugged. "No problem." He looked over towards the customer. She was tiny, even smaller than Miko, her dark curls bobbed, and her miniature face was hidden behind oversized sunglasses, even indoors. Her clothes were artfully selected, Finn could tell, vintage and faintly twee. She was tapping furiously on an iPad, then as Finn watched, she picked it up and took a photograph of the exposed brick walls of the restaurant.

Finn wandered over. "Hey there, I'm Finn Mason, the owner here. You're the girl that asked for kale chips?"

The young woman nodded. "I don't suppose it would be any trouble?"

"Not at all." He nodded at the iPad. "You like our place?"

She smiled at him, finally removing the sunglasses. Her face was like a porcelain doll, perfectly symmetrical. Her large brown eyes studied him. "I hope you don't mind. I run my own Instagram page and I like to document."

"Can I see?"

"Of course."

She handed him her iPad. He had to admit she had captured the atmosphere of his restaurant perfectly and even added a twist to it that he hadn't seen himself—it looked alive with energy. Underneath the photograph, she had written "*New favorite eatery on The Castro*."

And she hadn't even eaten anything yet. It occurred to him that she might have visited previously. "Have you been in before?"

"No, first time, but I have to say I'm very impressed."

He smiled at her. "Thanks for the recommendation. You do a lot of this stuff?"

She nodded and held out her hand. "Kenna Mitchell. Yes, this is my job. I use Instagram, YouTube, other sites to build up a picture of what's new and happening in modern culture. I keep my subscribers up to date on the latest trends." She looked around the restaurant. "Places like this with a young, hip feel."

*Young and hip.* Finn smiled. "Well, I didn't know we were that, but thank you."

"Are you kidding? Exposed brick walls, curated furnishings... you must have considered your client before you opened. And on The Castro too? Nicely done."

Finn was lost, but he nodded anyway. "Well, it's good to meet you. I'll get you those kale chips."

"I appreciate it."

Finn wandered back to the kitchen, slightly bemused and told Aiden about the newcomer. "*Curated* furniture, eh?" Aiden looked skeptical. "Did she mention the food?"

"Apart from asking about kale chips? Not as such."

Aiden harrumphed and, for a time, they worked side by side in silence. As Finn fried up a portion of kale—grinning at Aiden's eye rolling—he told him about the Instagram.

"So, she's an influencer?

"A what-o-what now?"

"*Grandpa.*" Aiden snickered as Finn flicked him with a dish cloth. "An influencer. People on the Internet who tell other people where to go, how to look, what to wear, etc. Now, that is useful to know."

"Why?"

"Lord, you are dumb as a bag of snakes."

Finn made a face. "It's mad as a bag of snakes, but okay. What's your point?"

"Social media, doofus. She might be able to guide us in the right direction. Maybe she knows someone who can help us out. Maybe she needs a job."

"And all she came in for was some kale chips."

"Hey, the kale chip girl?" David stuck his head in the kitchen, "She sends her apologies, but she had to run. She did pay for them, though."

Finn looked surprised. "Oh? Okay, well, there you go."

Aiden gave a little hiss. "Damn."

Finn shot his lover an amused look. "Dude, I'm sure there is more than one influencer out there we can exploit." He dumped the pan of kale chips onto a plate. "Now, who wants one?"

But later, at home, when Aiden had fallen asleep in his armchair—the *Grandpa Chair* as they had christened it—Finn searched 'Kenna Mitchell' on his laptop and found that she indeed did have a significant online presence. He found her video channel and began to watch. He had to give it to her, the videos were professionally produced, incredibly stylized and probably spoke to a certain section of the population but Finn wasn't sure it was his thing. However glossy they were, they were also a tad pretentious and a little patronizing too, on occasion.

"What's that?"

Aiden was awake now and watching over his shoulder. "Is this the girl from the restaurant?"

"Yep."

"Cute."

Finn looked at him askance and Aiden smiled. "If you like that sort of thing."

"What sort of thing?"

"Vagina." Aiden chortled as Finn made a face. "Sorry, I had to. I mean, they look pretty good, the videos."

"Uh-huh."

Aiden gave him a look. "What? What's that face for?"

"They look good, sure, but where's the substance? And doesn't it seem to be all about making *her* look good, rather than what she's recommending or whatever?"

Aiden shrugged, pulling up the chair next to him. "Well, maybe she is her brand."

"Fair enough but I've watched about seven of these things now and I still have no idea who she is or what she's selling."

"She's selling a way of life, an aesthetic. Social media is a visual art, K.B. Until they invent smell-o-vision or taste-o-vision, visuals are all we got. And she looks like she can produce some pretty professional shit. Maybe she can help us out."

Finn sat back in his chair. "You think so?"

Aiden shrugged. "Ah, what the hell do I know? But I think it's something we should consider. You know what else I think we should consider?"

"What's that?"

In answer, Aiden flicked up the bottom of Finn's t-shirt and pressed his lips against his flat stomach. Finn grinned, stroking his fingers through Aiden's thick blonde hair.

"Oh yeah?"

Aiden looked up. "Oh yeah."

"Feeling frisky?"

"Thinking about it."

They kissed, softly at first, then as the heat between them built, Aiden's lips were hungry against Finn's. "Sexy boy."

"Sweet talker." Finn felt Aiden's hands slide up under his t-shirt to his chest, his fingers brushing softly over the rough scar tissue. He tensed—no matter how many times Aiden touched him there, he couldn't help it—but Aiden smiled gently at him, leaning his forehead against his.

"S'okay, Boo."

He pressed his lips to Finn's neck, to the hollow of his throat and Finn closed his eyes. Letting his body relax, he ran his own hands under Aiden's shirt, bending to kiss his neck, his shoulder…

"Get your ass into the bedroom, dude."

Finn chuckled as Aiden pulled him to his feet. "You sure you want to? I mean, it's late and you're old, so…"

Aiden gave a growl and Finn, laughing, ducked away from him and went into the bedroom. "You want I should get the winch out?"

"Get your clothes *off*, boy, before this old man changes his mind."

And so, kissing and laughing, Finn did as he asked and they tumbled into bed, and held each other until dawn.

# Chapter Three

Three months after *Homefires* had opened, Finn walked into the kitchen one Friday morning to find Berto and Lisa yelling at each other. That was a surprise in itself—Finn had no idea the quiet Lisa *could* yell. And Berto, the comedian, never got mad. *Ever.*

"Woah, what the hell?"

Lisa saw Finn, turned scarlet and turned away from the men. Berto clammed up.

"What the hell is going on?"

Berto let out a deep sigh but said nothing, glaring at Lisa. Lisa stared down at her feet. Finn felt weird. *So, this is new…* Sure, in the heat of service, the cussing got bad and people snapped at each other, but he'd been lucky with the chemistry of his staff, the balance of the extroverted and introverted. Finn cleared his throat. "One of you. Speak up."

He felt like a parent or a school principal. "Lisa?"

Lisa sighed. "Nothing. I was talking to a customer, is all, and Berto got mad."

"You were *talking*? I heard you, Lisa, I *heard* you cuss her out."

"You cussed a customer out?" Finn really couldn't believe it. He looked between the two of them. Berto glared at Lisa some more. "Which customer?"

"I didn't see which customer it was, I just heard them yelling at each other. In front of the other diners."

Finn sighed. "Lisa?"

Lisa shifted from foot to foot. "It was nothing. I know... *knew* her from school, is all, and she's not the greatest person. She was rude to me and I snapped."

"Who?"

"It doesn't matter."

"Lisa."

She looked up at him, then, and Finn saw anger and resentment, and worryingly, a little fear, in her eyes. "It's nothing. Please Finn, just leave it." She looked at Berto, and her gaze softened. "I'm sorry, Berto, I didn't mean to yell. She just pushes my buttons, is all, and I should have let it go. I'm sorry Finn, it'll never happen again."

Finn nodded, considering. He'd let it go, too. It was so out of character for Lisa to be aggressive and, hell, it wasn't as if he didn't know what it was like to be bullied, to still carry the scars from that. Kids were *evil* in high school. "Okay, then. We have a service to get through guys, okay? You two up for it?"

"Sure, boss."

Berto didn't directly address Lisa but as Finn turned to his station, he saw Berto's hand briefly rub the back of Lisa's neck. Peace restored. Finn shook his head.

He turned his attention to his *mise en place*, chopping celery, onion, carrots for the *mirepoix,* gathering herbs, spices, and other seasonings, anything that they would need to prepare all the dishes, regardless of what orders came in. These were the staples without which no respectable kitchen would get through a service. Aiden was usually the one to do this, but this was a lunchtime sitting and Aiden was at home, sleeping off a migraine. Because of his no-drugs thing, he refused to even take Tylenol, and the debilitating migraines that had haunted him from his teenage years meant he was barely able to function when one hit. Finn knew Aiden would be irritated by having to waste a day in bed, but Finn shrugged it off. He'd get Jamie to step in as his sous-chef for the evening and hope they weren't too busy.

*Ha.* That was a joke. He yearned for them to be rushed off their feet. Okay, so, yes, their reputation was growing—their regular customers brought their friends, who in turn brought *their* friends and Finn was grateful for everyone who walked through the door, but it still felt like he was missing something.

And he knew what it was. He sighed. He hated marketing, loathed schmoozing and glad-handing, but in today's culture, an online presence was invaluable. The girl Finn had met hadn't been back to the restaurant, but he and Aiden had sought out some other media experts and today, after lunch service, Finn was meeting with a young woman who would be able to the handle that for them.

He finished up the *mise en place* then went to the cold store to check the deliveries for today. He noticed the fish delivery was missing. He stuck his head out of the door. "Hey, Berto, the fish guy not turn up?"

"He called. Says he's running an hour late."

Finn sighed. It would put prep back by an hour but what could he do? He went to the back door and tried to open it. The door jerked but only opened an inch and slammed back on him. "Fuck."

Berto looked up. "It's probably Old John again."

Old John was a hobo who lived in the alleyway at the back of the restaurant. Usually, he kept well clear of the door, out of respect for the business (and also because they fed him well) but when he got hold of some liquor, he was often too drunk to notice where he slept.

Finn went out the front of the restaurant and around to the alleyway. Sure enough, the big man was slumped against the door. "Hey, John."

John grumbled, still asleep. Finn slipped his arm under John's bulk and heaved him up. "Come on, buddy, you're blocking my kitchen." There was no malice there; every time Finn saw the man; he was reminded that this was nearly almost *his* own life. John was a kind, intelligent man who'd once been a university lecturer. Life was a bitch, sometimes.

John barely woke as Finn moved him to a less inconvenient spot. Finn grabbed one of John's filthy blankets and draped it over the sleeping man. John hated any kind of charity—except food—and so Finn knew it was useless to offer him clean clothes or blankets or anything. "*Naw*, man," John would say, "I'll take your food, but anything else I gotta get for myself."

As Finn went back into the restaurant, the lunchtime crowd was beginning to gather. The service passed without any trouble—even the fish guy turned up earlier than expected—and after eating with the staff, Finn went out into the restaurant to wait for the social media expert.

He saw Lisa take off down the hill and wondered again what her problem with the customer had been. He was inclined to take Lisa's side—she wasn't one for making trouble out of nowhere.

"Boss, I'm taking off now."

"Thanks, Berto. See you tonight."

"Sure will. Good luck with the tech nerd."

Finn grinned at his friend. "Thanks, buddy."

An hour later and Finn was checking his text messages, while he waited for his interviewee. The woman, Carrie Goss, was forty-five minutes late and Finn was getting pissed. There was no message telling him she'd be late or that she'd cancelled. When it got to an hour after the allotted appointment, he called her. "Hey, Carrie."

"Hey, Mr. Mason, how are you doing? Did you change your mind?"

Finn frowned. "I'm sorry?"

"About meeting me? Your secretary called and said you'd gone another way. It's fine, of course, but it *was* rather short notice."

"My what?... Carrie, I don't have a secretary. I've been waiting at *Homefires* for an hour for you to show up."

There was a silence on the other end of the line. "Mr. Mason, I'm confused. I got a call, this morning, from a woman telling me that she was your assistant and that you needed to cancel my appointment."

Finn was bewildered. "This is... weird. Are you sure she said she was my assistant? Not another of your clients?"

When Carrie Goss spoke again, her voice was distinctly cooler. "Mr. Mason, I'm not an idiot. I heard her say the words *I am Mr. Mason's assistant.* Homefires will not be requiring your services. Now, with respect, unless you are calling to offer me another appointment..."

"No, I'm sorry. There must have been a mix-up."

"Clearly."

Finn grimaced. "I'm sorry I wasted your time."

He ended the call and sat back. *What the actual hell?*

It was still bugging him as he drove home. The apartment was quiet and dark as he went inside. He went straight to the bedroom to find the blackout blinds still drawn and Aiden lying prone on the bed, the covers pushed back. Finn was about to leave him alone, but then he heard him speak.

"I'm awake, K.B."

Finn perched on the end of the bed and ran his hand over Aiden's clammy forehead. "How are you feeling?"

"Rough as fuck but at least the nausea's gone. Maybe I could come in tonight."

"No, man, stay in bed. We got it covered. Want something to eat?"

Aiden shook his head and winced. "Bad idea."

"It might help. Maybe some soup, a hunk of that honey loaf we got from the deli?"

Aiden considered. "I'll give it a go."

Finn went to the bathroom and filled a glass of cold water. "Here. This will help too. Be right back."

He warmed up some soup for Aiden and cut up some bread. As he worked, he tried to make sense of what had happened this afternoon, and his confusion must have shown on his face when he took the tray of food into Aiden, because his lover narrowed his eyes at him.

"S'up? You look hinky."

Finn told him what had happened. "She was so sure it was my personal assistant, is all. I don't get it."

"Maybe she's a little nuts?"

Finn grinned. "Maybe *you* are. Ah, what does it matter? Just means we have to start over again."

"Maybe it's a sign we should forget it."

Finn shook his head. "No, we need to do this. You're right—if we want the young and hip clientele—and ugh, I hate even saying it like that, then we have to have an online presence."

Aiden—who'd practically scarfed down the soup and bread, set the tray aside. "Come lay down with me. I'll show you young and hip."

Finn snorted. "Right. Is that before or after you upchuck that soup on me, old man?"

Aiden grinned and rested his head back against the headboard. "You might be right. It might be overambitious. Compromise? Come nap with me a while."

"That," Finn said, kicking off his sneakers, "I can do."

He laid down next to Aiden and pulled his lover's head onto his chest. Aiden's arm snaked around his waist. "Before you know it," Aiden said, his voice partially muffled by Finn's t-shirt, "we're going to be one of those old couples whose greatest wish is just to have an early night and cuddle."

"I think we're already there, dude. Now, close your eyes. Let this other old man get some rest."

# Chapter Four

Aiden was well enough to return to work for the next lunchtime service and as Finn read out the tickets for the orders, Aiden nodded at him. "Getting busier."

"I think so too."

As service progressed, Finn took a moment to stick his head around the door to the front of the house. As he suspected, the place was packed and, for the first time, he saw people lining up, waiting to be seated. A thrill went through him. "Be right back," he said to Aiden, who nodded.

Sarah, their evening hostess, was working the afternoon shift for extra cash and she beamed at Finn as he approached. "Lookit." She gestured to the queue of people.

"I know, right? Maybe we're starting to get some traction."

"Maybe. I asked a couple of people where they had heard of us and some of them said they'd seen a review of us online. I pulled it up. Take a look."

She handed Finn her iPad. Finn watched the video—it was brief, and had mostly stylized shots of the interior of the place with a couple of shots thrown in of his more artistic dishes. Towards the end, there were shots of Kenna Mitchell, dressed up like a china doll, sipping tea and talking directly to camera, quoting poetry, and smiling into the lens as the camera tilted at an angle. It was all faintly ridiculous but Sarah pointed at the number of views and Finn boggled.

"And they came because of *this*?"

"So it would seem." Sarah looked up. "And your auteur is among them." She nodded over to one of the couches and Finn saw Kenna holding court with a group of younger people. She sensed his scrutiny and smiled. Finn walked over.

"Hello again."

"Hi." She got up and, to Finn's bemusement, she kissed both of his cheeks. She turned to her companions. "This is the man, everyone. Finn Mason. Owner and head-chef."

To Finn's embarrassment, she then burst into applause as did her friends. Other diners shot them amused glances as Finn's face burned scarlet.

"Well," he said, "well."

"Listen," Kenna drew him to one side, "I hope you don't mind my little video. I know I probably overstepped a little, and I hope I didn't infringe any copyrights, but when I get inspired, my creativity just has to have an outlet."

Finn smiled, nodding at the line of people waiting to get in. "Listen, if you have half to do with that, there's no problem. Thanks… it is very much appreciated."

"You're welcome."

"Listen… could you spare some time after the lunchtime rush? There's a few things I'd like to talk to you about."

Kenna nodded, smiling, and there was a hint of smugness to it.

"Of course."

Finn made his way back to the kitchen. As he opened the door, he saw his staff—Aiden, Berto, Miko, Clyde and Jamie—standing watching him in silence.

"What?"

They looked at each other and then burst into loud, mocking applause. Finn grinned, giving them the finger. "Oh, very fucking funny."

"Would his majesty like a hot towel?" Aiden lobbed a damp dish-cloth into Finn's face.

Berto dipped into a deep curtsy. "Or perhaps he would like some grapes peeled?"

Even Jamie, the quiet Englishman, got in on the act. "Or his balls gently flambéed?"

"You're all fired. Get back to work." But he was grinning. Somehow even their mockery felt like a victory.

Aiden nudged him. "Now that, my friend, is a shit-eating grin."

"You know what, loser? I think today might just be a good one."

* * *

Kenna was waiting patiently for them as Finn and Aiden finished cleaning up. Finn introduced the young woman and saw Aiden sizing her up. He could tell what his lover was thinking—this kid was way too pretentious, way too… stylized for him.

He had to admit she did seem a little *too* put together. The clothes looked vintage but, seeing them up close, the fabric was too modern to be authentic, and her make-up, although expertly applied, was crafted so that it gave her a vaguely exotic look which he doubted was genuine. Her nose was contoured to look smaller than it was, and her large brown eyes were watchful. She noticed his scrutiny and smiled, although it didn't reach her eyes. "Is something wrong?"

"Not at all." Finn felt his face flame red and hurried to assuage the awkwardness. "So, listen, we wanted to say we're really grateful to you for making that video."

"You're welcome. Like I told you when we me:, I like to support people and places in the city that I think could make an impact." She looked around. "The exposed brick, the couches, the way it's cool and hip and yet relaxed… yeah. I can see it."

Finn felt Aiden shift in his chair. "What about the food?"

"The food is great."

Aiden's eyebrows shot up. "Is that all?"

Kenna smiled coolly. "What else do you want me to say?"

Finn decided to intervene before Aiden got snippy. "What Aiden means is… yes, our…" He cast around for the right word.

"Aesthetic," Kenna said.

"Yes. Our *aesthetic* is everything you say but our focus is the food. What we serve, how customers react and why more should come to eat here. Listen, let's get down to it. How would you feel about handling our social media presence?"

Kenna didn't seem surprised by the offer. "I could do that… are we talking a full-time position?"

"If we need that."

Kenna considered. "I would need somewhere to work."

"You could do it from home."

"If I'm going to be here to really capture the ambiance, then I do need access. Photos of the kitchen, the food, the customers." She smiled. "I need access to you two, your stories. Have I got it right? You're a couple, yes?"

Finn nodded, but he heard Aiden sigh. He wasn't convinced; he could tell. Finn ignored him. "There are offices you can work from upstairs."

"Good. Listen, let me get together a proposal and a budget I can work with and I'll get back to you." Kenna glanced at her watch. "Listen, I do have another appointment this afternoon." She took a business card out of her purse. "I'll let you know as soon as possible."

And then she was gone, leaving Finn holding her card. He looked at Aiden who grinned. "Well, we sure let her know who's in charge around here."

"You think we've made a mistake?"

"You, dude, you. This was *your* idea. I don't know yet."

Finn narrowed his eyes at Aiden to cover the fact he was embarrassed. Kenna had ridden roughshod over him and he knew it. "What did you think of her? Really?"

"Style over substance—and if anything about her is genuine, I'd be surprised."

"Harmless, though, right?"

"We'll see."

It was at home, much later after evening service that Aiden called Finn over to him. His laptop was open. "Look at this."

Finn looked over his shoulder. A Facebook page dedicated to *Homefires* was open, and Finn read through the blurb on it. The page already had a few hundred '*Likes*' despite the lack of photographs. The ones on the timeline were the same that Kenna had used for her video, but the page looked good, Finn had to admit.

Aiden glanced at him. "Look at this." He indicated the blurb at the side of the page.

*Kenna Mitchell, Executive Social Media Consultant, Homefires.*

"I guess she took the job then."

"Nice of her to let us know."

As if on cue, Finn's cellphone bleeped. "She sent an entire document." He browsed through it. "Huh."

"What?"

"Did we talk about pay?"

"We hardly did any of the talking. What's she asking for?"

Finn showed him the contract and Aiden whistled. "Is that the going rate?"

"How would I know?"

"Can we afford her?"

Finn sighed. "I guess. If she brings in the clientele like she did today…"

"Then make it on a trial basis." Aiden swung around in his chair to face his lover. "Make her pay profit-based."

"That's a good idea." Finn put his phone down and Aiden raised his eyebrows. "What?"

"You not gonna text her back?"

"Not tonight. Let her stew for a minute. Besides…" he nodded at the computer screen, "she's already started the job we haven't confirmed yet. That's free advertising right there."

Aiden grinned. "So very cut-throat. I love it."

Finn bent to kiss him. "Come show me how much."

In bed, they wrestled and laughed and kissed each other in every place, before making love slowly. Aiden kissed the back of Finn's neck as they fucked and Finn closed his eyes, taking in a deep breath as he relaxed his body, letting the sweet sensations flood through him.

With Aiden, it had always been like this, the meeting of two bodies that fitted together so perfectly, the fact they had this instinctive knowledge of what the other liked, what they didn't.

Aiden was only Finn's second lover and, every day, Finn thanked the universe for finding him. After what had happened when he was younger, back in Kansas, he had thought he would never be able to love anyone—certainly, not trust them—and for Finn, those two came hand in hand. There was no love without trust.

When he'd found Aiden, to an outsider, it would have seemed that Aiden was the fucked-up one. His Vicodin and alcohol addictions were at their pinnacle or their nadir, whichever way you looked at it, and the night Finn found him beaten and bleeding in the alleyway had been the turning point.

They'd fallen in love quickly, but Finn hadn't been easy on him. "You get clean or I'm done."

It took those six simple, heartfelt words, for Aiden to turn his life around. Finn knew Aiden loved him when he voluntarily checked himself into rehab for a six-week stay. When he came out, Aiden introduced Finn to his stunned family. Aiden's father, Glenn, an austere, grey-haired man who had made his money in real estate had cried, had actually burst into noisy sobs and hugged Finn to him like a son.

That had been a new feeling, and it was more than a little disconcerting to a young man who had been more or less discarded by most of his own family. That moment changed Finn for good.

He and Aiden moved in together but New York kept trying to lure Aiden back to his past life and eventually he told Finn he couldn't do it. "I need a change of scenery, baby. A new life."

They'd kicked around a few ideas—Finn had nixed the idea of going back to Kansas right away and Aiden assured him he hadn't been serious at the suggestion. Then, at a lunch thrown by Aiden's family, his father had proposed that he bankroll a restaurant for them. "Anywhere you like. Somewhere you can start again."

San Francisco was the obvious—some would say, clichéd—choice for a gay couple, but as soon as Finn and Aiden rode into the city on Aiden's Harley, they knew it was the right one.

Just before Finn fell asleep, Aiden kissed him. "We're winning, you know?" He said the words softly, almost as if he couldn't quite believe it, but Finn smiled.

"I know," he said, "you and me, baby."

"You and me. Always."

# Chapter Five

Kenna looked around the open office space above the restaurant. As Finn and Aiden watched, she moved to each of the windows overlooking the Bay. Aiden shot Finn an amused look. She hadn't spoken for the last five minutes except to say she was "absorbing".

Finn couldn't tell if Aiden was amused or irritated, but Finn shrugged. If this was the woman's thing, what did it matter? All he cared about was if she could help his business.

He'd emailed her back the following day after she'd sent through her requirements.

"*Demands.*" Aiden had said, darkly, but Finn grinned.

"Just because she demands, doesn't mean we have to agree."

In the end, they had reached a compromise. A three-month contract at eighty percent of what Kenna had originally quoted, with an option to extend if things went well. Kenna had agreed and now, a week later, she was upstairs at *Homefires*, choosing her working 'space.'

"This is good. It has a nice *chi* to it." She put her brown leather messenger bag down on a table. "Here, I think." She reached into the messenger bag and pulled out a small cactus, nestled inside a Louboutin shoe. She placed it carefully on the table.

Finn saw Aiden roll his eyes. "That's fine. Now, we should talk strategy."

"Oh, I have a plan." She waved her hand around, almost dismissing them, but Finn wasn't having that.

"No, I think we need to discuss the restaurant's requirements and what Aiden and I want going forward. For *our* restaurant, you understand." There was a steel to his voice that made two spots of pink appear high on Kenna's face, but she nodded.

"Of course. I just meant I have some ideas to discuss with you."

"Good, well, I think the best thing for now is to introduce you to the staff."

Kenna followed them down to the kitchen. It was late afternoon and kitchen prep had already begun. Finn introduced Kenna to Berto, Clyde, Miko and Jamie and then looked around for Lisa.

"She's not in, boss. Called to say she was sick. Clyde's taking over her station."

Finn's lips pursed. "Really?"

Berto nodded. "Don't stress, we got it covered."

Kenna was watching the exchange carefully. "Man down already?"

"It's fine. I'll show you how each station works, you can take photos and ask the staff anything—as long as you don't interfere with the service. Also, after service, we all have dinner together. Up to you whether you want to stay?"

"I'd like that."

"Good. Well, we're deep into prep so make yourself at home."

Finn felt a little awkward but Kenna merely nodded and moved around the kitchen, talking to everyone and photographing the various stages of prep.

Aiden pulled Finn aside when he saw her deep in conversation with Jamie. "How's it going?"

"Unclear as yet. She's not getting in the way so that's a good start." Finn studied Aiden's expression. "You're still not convinced, are you?"

"I just think… oh hell, I don't know. All this hipster shit is a bit young for me."

Finn grinned at him and Aiden chuckled. "I know—*Grandpa*."

Finn shot a look over at Kenna. "Listen, if it brings in more customers, what does it matter? If she wants to parade around like she's…" He cast around looking for a name. "Christ, I don't know. But if that's her thing, so be it. I remember when your thing was stonewash and paisley."

"Hey, never knock paisley. That bandanna was…"

"Gross. We had to burn it."

"Well, okay, yeah." Aiden poked Finn's side. "It was from my Axl Rose phase."

Finn gave an exaggerated shudder. "Don't remind me. Also, you know your Axl Rose phase was about thirty years after everyone else's?"

Aiden grinned. "I was being ironic."

Finn groaned and elbowed Aiden out of his way. "I'm leaving you."

"Who for?"

"A Jonas brother."

"Now, that *is* insulting. Also, so 2006."

They continued to rib each other as they prepared for the evening service and soon, Kenna's artful manner was far from their minds. She did as they asked, stayed out of the way, but drifted around, taking photographs and asking questions.

Finn, waiting for orders to come in, decided to take the trash out. Even now, as the big boss, he didn't mind doing it—it was a task that fell to whoever wasn't busy at a particular time in his kitchen, even him. He grabbed the bag and tried to open the back door.

"Aw, dang it, John."

"What's up?"

Kenna had appeared behind him. Finn smiled and shrugged. "Nothing. We've an old homeless guy, lives in the alley. Usually he's no trouble, but he must have gotten hold of some booze. He's sleeping against the door."

Kenna smiled and held her hand out. Finn frowned then realized she was offering to take the trash. "I'll move him along."

Finn looked at her askance. Kenna could only be a hundred pounds, if that. John was three times her size. "No, it's okay."

"If you're sure."

A few moments later, he was helping John up. "Hey, buddy, we doing this again?"

"Sorry, boss. Some kid left a bottle of Absinthe."

"Jeez, John."

"I know." John grinned suddenly at Finn. "Best stuff I been left for a while now. Actually made a dent in the old noggin." He tapped his head and chuckled.

"John… you be careful what you take from people. There are

sickos out there who'd put battery acid in booze bottles just to hurt you."

John waved him away, then slumped into his bed of old boxes and half-destroyed blankets. "Buddy, I'm good, I've got street smarts. I can take care of myself. You're a good kid."

Finn went back into the restaurant. Kenna smiled at him. "All clear?"

"All clear. How's it going?"

Kenna showed him the photos she had taken and Finn had to admit the girl had an eye. "I might disappear upstairs and work for a while," she said to him. "I have an idea to post some teaser shots to the Facebook page then do an entire article on the day-to-day of the restaurant."

"Sounds good to me." Finn was already onto other things in his head and he didn't even notice her going back to her office.

Evening service kicked in early. It was a Friday and people wanted to eat before they went to the clubs, Finn knew, but to his surprise and delight, his clientele wasn't just the young crowd, but people of all ages who came to the restaurant—older, gay couples who wanted somewhere to eat and relax, hetero couples, singles. He was even pleased to see an elderly couple holding hands while they ate, sitting at the table near the window. He said as much to Aiden.

"You realize that's us in ten years."

Finn hid a grin. "No, dude, that's me in ten years, that's you right *now*."

"Anyone tell you you're a bitch?"

Finn laughed. "Only you. Seriously, though, I love to see that."

Aiden smiled at him. "You're still that Kansas boy, you know?

Wanting to provide a safe space for everyone."

Finn shrugged. "I don't deny it." He hesitated for a moment. "After… what happened, all I wanted was somewhere to go that wouldn't judge me—would just say, hey you know, it's okay to be *you*." He flushed. "I'm not arrogant enough to say we're *that*, yet, but I hope we could be."

"Is this a restaurant or a refuge?"

"Why can't it be both?"

Aiden touched Finn's face and smiled. "This. *This* is why I love you. Don't ever change, K.B. I just… I never want you to be hurt again, you know? You see things in black and white a lot of the time and mostly, that's okay."

"Just mostly?"

Aiden shrugged. "Even after everything, I worry your heart can be too open. Idealism can get you hurt when you least expect it."

Finn smiled and kissed him. "I know."

"But do you though, honey?" Aiden leaned his forehead against Finn's. "Still my Kansas boy."

"Still him."

They turned back to their work, still ribbing each other, and it wasn't until a brief lull in orders that Finn heard Kenna's voice.

"Why does he call you K.B.?"

He turned around to see her leaning against the door to the stairs. She had very watchful eyes, he thought. This girl didn't miss much. "It's short for Kansas Boy."

"Ah. Whereabouts?"

"Whitewater. You know Kansas?"

She shook her head. "No, not at all. I was just curious."

Finn glanced at the clock. "You know, you don't have to be here this late." It was already half-past nine, but Kenna shrugged.

"I like being here. I like the energy."

He smiled at her. "Fair enough."

"I won't get in the way."

"I didn't think you would. You haven't so far. How's the strategy planning going?"

Kenna smiled. "Getting there. I'm just setting up all the social media accounts for you. I didn't realize you didn't have *any* online presence."

She sounded vaguely appalled which made Finn chuckle. "It's just not my kind of thing, our kind of thing, is all. I'm busy with the restaurant, with making sure we have the right produce, the right staff… heck, you know. I'm not good with that kind of thing. Aiden's even worse. We're older than you, Kenna."

She came closer, studying him intently and Finn flushed. "You're what? Thirty?"

"Thirty-two."

"You're hardly old. Don't you want to be recognized? Don't you want to be feted by your peers?"

Finn could smell her perfume now, even over the scents of the kitchen. Floral, slightly cloying. Too much vanilla, he thought. Something else he'd noticed: Kenna had no idea about personal space. She was standing way too close now but, not wanting to hurt her feelings, he turned to grab a pair of tongs and took a step away from her. When he looked back, there was a sly smile on Kenna's face and he knew he was busted. *She didn't miss a thing, did she?*

"So, you've set up some accounts?" He hoped his face wasn't

burning, but thankfully, she went into what she'd done. Aiden walked over while she was talking, listening to her carefully.

"Seems kind of obvious. I'm just saying: Facebook, Twitter? What are we paying you for?"

Finn shot Aiden a loaded look but Kenna shrugged. "Yes, obvious choices. So why weren't they already set up? Why wasn't it the first thing you did even before opening the restaurant? Do you realize how big your opening could have been with even just one Facebook ad, one viral Tweet?"

She had a smile on her face, but her stare challenged Aiden to come back at her.

"That told *you*." Finn muttered, and heard Aiden tutting something under his breath before he moved away. Finn grinned at Kenna. "Like I said, social media isn't really our thing."

Later, when Kenna had finally left, and the restaurant was closed, clean-up was underway, and Finn went to find Aiden. "Man, you really don't like Kenna, huh?"

"It's not that I don't like her, it's that she's been here an entire day and all she's done is set up a Facebook page and a Twitter account?"

Finn sighed. He looked around, "Hey, Berto? You got this down here? Me and Aiden need to go check on something."

"Sure, boss. Almost done."

Finn and Aiden went up to the office, flicking on the lights. "Oh."

The entire office furniture had been rearranged. "Well, I guess she *was* busy today."

Finn sighed and went to the computer, firing it up. "Who cares? It looks better this way."

He opened a browser and typed in the name and location of the restaurant. Just as Kenna told them, the results page showed *Facebook*, *Twitter* and *Instagram* accounts for the restaurants. Finn clicked on the first link. "Woah."

Aiden came to look over his shoulder. "Well… okay, I take it back."

The *Facebook* page was full of photographs, stylized in the extreme, but all of them showing the restaurant in full flow, capturing the hustle of the kitchen perfectly. Images of diners laughing and joking—although Finn did notice the people Kenna captured were all young and hip, rather than the eclectic clientele the restaurant had begun to host, but they could work on that.

"This looks pretty cool."

Aiden was squinting at the screen. "Look at the comments."

Finn scanned through the posts on the page, and a small thrill went through him.

*Love this place!*

*Great food, a great hang-out spot.*

*My new favorite place on The Castro.*

"Are you seeing this?"

"Dude, it's one, two… six comments. Don't get too excited but yeah, I have to admit, it's a start." Aiden put his arms around Finn's neck, rested his chin on top of Finn's head. "Hey… did you see that?"

He pointed to the sidebar. Finn read it. Page curated by Kenna Mitchell, Chief Marketing Executive, Homefires.

"Fancy title she gave herself."

Finn shrugged. "I don't care what she calls herself if she gets the clients in and raises our profile."

Aiden tugged Finn's head back gently and kissed his forehead. "Let's go home and go to bed. I'll *curate* some extra special moves just for you."

Finn grinned. "Now you're talking." He flicked off the laptop and took another look around the office space. Despite his initial nonchalance, there was a slight annoyance that Kenna had taken it upon herself to change the office around as she did… but then again, she was the person who would be using it mostly, so what did it matter?

They locked up the restaurant and got onto Aiden's Harley. Neither of them saw the small figure waiting in the shadows across the street. As the motorbike's taillights disappeared down Castro, she moved quickly to the restaurant's door and let herself in, melting into the shadows of the darkened, silent building.

# Chapter Six

Finn let the call go to voicemail again. He hissed to himself, shaking his head. Once again, Lisa hadn't shown up to work and his kitchen was understaffed. His crew took the news with a good-humored shrug and although the line was working well together to make up for the shortfall, Finn's tension was up.

It was Friday, and the restaurant was full, with, for the first time, a wait list and the knowledge that they were finally gaining traction was making Finn feel both elated and nervous. He was never gladder of everyone, his employees, his *friends*, in the kitchen as they worked, laughing and busting each other's balls. But the fact his once-trusted chef Lisa was M.I.A. was weighing on his mind.

Berto and Clyde weren't about to let him stew in his own annoyance though. They teased him mercilessly throughout service.

Finn snagged the tickets from the order machine.

"Order up, Berto! Three of the salmon, Clyde. Two of the duck, one steak: table seven."

"*Oui*, Chef!"

Finn grinned. "Cut that out."

"*Oui*, Chef!"

"Jerks." But he chuckled.

Only Jamie was quiet and withdrawn, Finn noticed, and in a lull in service, he pulled the young Englishman aside and asked him what was going on.

"It's Lisa. Has she called you at all to tell you why she hasn't shown up for work?"

"No... I tried to call her cell phone a few times. It isn't like her, I know, but I'm not her keeper, buddy."

Jamie studied him. "You're right, it *isn't* like her. So... God, I went to her place. Finn, the landlord said the place has been empty for the last three days; there's no sign of her. He let me in. All of her stuff is still there but there's no sign of Lisa anywhere."

Jamie's voice was getting louder, and he stopped, checked himself. "I'm not usually like this," he confessed, giving Finn a sheepish smile, "but this is bloody weird."

Finn noticed his cheeks had colored. "Jamie, you and Lisa?"

"We've sort of been seeing each other—nothing heavy—but there was something there." There was the faintest quiver to Jamie's voice, and he stopped himself embarrassed. "Finn, Lisa loves working here. *Loves* it. She told me that she had spent her whole career trying to get to a place like this, with bosses and colleagues who didn't look down on her for being a woman in a kitchen. You know what male chefs can be like."

"Don't I just?" Finn rubbed his head. "Look, let's get service out of the way and I'll try to get in touch with her."

"Please. She hasn't got any family in the city I can call. It's weird, Finn."

So now, Finn was in the office, repeatedly trying to call Lisa's cell. He called one final time before her voicemail told him it was full. Finn shook his head. He'd spent time finding the most talented chefs he could for the restaurant and now he'd have to put extra work into finding someone new.

Somewhere, a toilet flushed and he looked up, frowning. It was after midnight and when the restroom door opened and Kenna emerged, Finn raised his eyebrows at her. "Hey… you know what time it is, right?"

She gave him a half-smile. "I know."

"I like the dedication, but it is after midnight." He studied her. "Kenna… is something going with you? I mean, is there a reason you can't go home?"

"Not at all…" But then her shoulders slumped, and she sighed. "Just some personal stuff."

"Do you want to talk about it?"

She shook her head. "No, I'm fine. Work helps."

"Well, you are doing a great job so far."

"Really, it's nothing. I have so much planned that I'd like to discuss with you at some point."

Finn smiled at her. "Any time. Give me a preview."

"Well," she pulled up a chair next to him, "I was thinking about how we could improve the aesthetics of the place. I think you've done a great job with the interior, but we also need to think about the exterior."

"You mean like signage?" Finn was a little stung—he and Aiden had spent time and way too much money on the bespoke wooden sign that hung over the door of the restaurant. They'd driven up to

Oregon to source it from a craftsman Aiden had heard about online and the moment it had been finished was the moment it had hit Finn that *Homefires* was a reality and not just a dream any more.

Kenna smiled. "No, not the signage. I'm talking about the alleyway behind the restaurant. Why does it have to be the clichéd dark alley with a built-in transient? We could move him along, and make it a safe space for anyone needing to use the passageway. I know we can't do anything about the dumpsters, but even then, we could get some bespoke cabins made to hide the dumpsters away."

Finn frowned at her. "Kenna… what?"

"The homeless guy. We need to ask him to move along."

"To *where,* Kenna? The alleyway does not belong to the restaurant, it is a public throughway, and even so…"

"You're encouraging him to stay, feeding him, giving him free stuff all the time. We need to be rid of him if this restaurant is going to be held up as the pinnacle of fine dining on The Castro."

Finn shook his head in disbelief. "Not an option, Kenna. God. Don't you think John has it hard enough?"

Kenna muttered something that sounded like "So, it has a name?" and Finn gritted his teeth.

"It isn't within your remit, Kenna. Drop it."

"Fine." She shrugged. "I'm just saying. You hired me to look at aesthetics…"

"We hired you to improve our social media presence."

"It goes hand in hand."

Finn's eyes narrowed. "No, Kenna, it doesn't. We want substance over style… I thought you recognized that."

But now that he said, had he ever said as much to her? Had he been clear with her? "Look, go home. We'll talk more tomorrow about what Aiden and I need for our business."

Kenna shrugged, seemingly not affected by his mood. "Okay." She snagged her bag from the back of Finn's chair and threw him a wave as she went out of the door. The room rang with silence afterward and Finn went to the window. Down on the street, he saw Kenna walking quickly to the top of the street, towards the tram stop. He felt a little irritated but also concerned she was alone at this time of night. He should have ordered her a cab at the very least.

The computer was still on and Finn wheeled himself closer and tapped the mouse on his emails. He scanned down the list of senders, looking for any messages from Lisa. In among the many spam emails, he saw the one without a sender. He clicked on it, expecting some kind of scam, but when he read the single sentence, a small thrill of adrenaline spiked through him. He checked it over carefully, and although his first response was that this was about his missing chef, it was with a growing certainty that Finn re-read the simple message and knew, deep down, it had something to do with Kenna Mitchell. One simple sentence.

Don't trust her.

* * *

Aiden squinted over at Finn. His lover was zoned out, even as they sat in the ocean-side restaurant on Cannery Row. Aiden had suggested the day trip to Monterey as a way to get far away from the stress of running the restaurant but he could tell, even now, Finn's mind was back on Castro. "Dude, seriously… we get *one* day off in a week. Be present, please."

"Sorry, baby."

Finn leaned across the table and kissed Aiden. Aiden grinned back. Even a year ago, Finn was reluctant to even hold hands in public. Aiden wound his fingers in between Finn's now as they waited for their food. Finn nodded out to the swell of the Pacific, the white heads of the waves crashing against the rocks.

"Man, can you imagine living somewhere like this?"

"You like it, huh?"

Finn nodded. "Maybe, if we can grow the business, we could open up a second restaurant here."

"Maybe."

They sat in companionable silence as they ate—mahi-mahi in a warm peanut sauce with rice for Finn, swordfish *Del Mar* for Aiden. Over coffee afterward, Finn looked around the restaurant's decor. The high ceilings were sealed and oiled reclaimed hardwood, with the light fittings artsy tangled metal constructions. At the back of the bar, the brickwork was exposed with old gas fittings retro-fitted. The floor-to-ceiling windows afforded glorious views over the ocean.

"Kenna would have a field day in here."

"Huh."

Finn looked at Aiden. "You're still not convinced by her, are you?"

Aiden shrugged. "I just think there's very little depth to the girl. And she has this look on her face all the time…" He pulled his lips together in a prissy moue, tilted his head to one side and stared without blinking and Finn nearly choked on his soda. Aiden had captured Kenna's simper exactly and now he crossed his eyes and nodded to the bar. "I just adore the simple wainscoting, the weft of the wood, the simple and yet complex way the barkeep flicks his moustache."

Finn shook his head, laughing. "That's so mean but so…"

"So *Kenna.*" Aiden put his hands under his chin and fluttered his eyelashes. Finn snorted.

"Stop."

"I'm right, though."

Finn smiled, nodding. "You have her down. *Weft* of the wood? Do you even know what you're talking about?"

"Nope, but then neither does Kenna." Aiden sighed. "I just … hell, Finn, she's pretentious … and there's something else."

"What?" Finn studied his partner curiously. "What is it?"

Aiden picked up his beer and took a sip before answering. "She gives me the heebs."

Finn smoothed out his expression and nodded sagely. "So," he said slowly, "big old Aiden Fox is scaredy-waredy of a little girl."

"Fuck off." Aiden was grinning, as Finn winked at him.

"A tiny, whiny *ickle* girl…"

"Screw you, Mason."

"Promises." Finn smirked, then as the waitress came over to bring their check, he leaned forward and whispered. "Just so happens… there's a pier along the beach there, lots of secret places, lots of discreet large poles to hide behind."

"Mason, we're too old to go screw behind a post."

"Are we?"

Aiden's answering grin was wide and lascivious. "Hell, no. Get your ass down there right *now.*"

On the way back to San Francisco, Finn wrapped his arms around Aiden's back as the Harley weaved between the traffic, leaning his head against Aiden's back. He'd been right—they had needed this time away, even for a day, to remember that not everything was all business, all the time. They could afford to kick back a little.

Still, as the bike took them into Castro, he couldn't resist looking at the darkened restaurant. For a second, he thought he saw a light burning in the window on the second floor, but as Aiden pulled the bike to a stop at the red light, Finn looked back and there was nothing but darkness. He shrugged and looked away as the light turned green and Aiden sped away.

* * *

At four a.m. Finn's phone began to buzz. He ignored it at first, being as comfortable as he was wrapped around Aiden's body, but when it wouldn't quit, he gave an annoyed grunt and rolled over, reaching out to the nightstand.

"'lo?"

"Finn?"

Finn sat up in bed. *Jamie.* Jamie never called him. *Ever.* "Jamie, what is it?"

"Finn, mate… it's Lisa." His voice sounded hollow. "She's dead."

The shock was icy cold and constricting. "What?"

"They pulled her body out of the Bay. The police are here."

"Where are you?"

His young colleague sounded flat. "The restaurant. Can you come?"

"Yes, of course. God… Jamie…"

"I know."

"We'll be there as soon as we can."

# Chapter Seven

Finn wasn't prepared for the look of utter shock and desolation on Jamie's face as they walked into *Homefires*. The police were there, several detectives talking to his staff and as he entered, the lead detective introduced himself. "Hal Fields. Are you the owners?"

Finn introduced himself and Aiden. "This is about Lisa?"

"I'm afraid so. We identified the body of a young woman pulled from the Bay last night as Lisa Armitage. I understand she works… worked… here?"

"Since we opened. Detective, what happened?"

"You notice any strange behavior from Miss Armitage the last time you saw her?"

Finn and Aiden exchanged a glance. "She didn't show up for work the last two days. I tried to call her but…"

"Yeah, we got a record of your calls to her voice mail."

"You found her phone?"

The detective hesitated. "We found Miss Armitage's possessions placed neatly at a site on the bridge."

"Golden Gate?" Finn didn't even know why he asked the

question; what did it matter? Lisa was gone. He felt the backs of his eyes burning.

"Yes." The detective looked at him curiously. "We found her wallet, her I.D., her phone."

Aiden cleared his throat. "So… you think it was a suicide?"

"We can't say that for certain yet, but looks like it. I'm sorry for your loss."

Finn looked over at Jamie: the young man looked as if he would pass out any moment. "Excuse me a moment, detective."

"Of course."

Finn went to his side. Jamie looked at him and just shook his head. Finn put his arm around his shoulders.

"I don't get it. Why the fuck would she…? Jesus Christ." Jamie dropped his head into his hands. "I don't know if I can handle this, Finn, I really don't."

Finn wished he had some words of comfort for him, but the shock was so raw, so absolute. Berto and Clyde were sitting together, talking in hushed tones, both looking wretched and Miko was stone-faced and pale. One of their own was dead.

There was a small commotion at the door and Finn went over. Kenna was outside, looking annoyed. "Finn, will you tell these morons to let me in? I *work* here."

"She does." He waved Kenna in and looked at the officer. "I'm sorry, dudes. She doesn't know."

"No problem."

Finn went back inside to see Aiden talking to Kenna. Kenna was nodding along. As Finn joined them, he heard her say "Was she always unbalanced?"

Aiden rocked back and Finn's hands clenched. "Kenna, Lisa wasn't *unbalanced* and please, don't talk about her that way."

"I'm sorry, that came out wrongly. I apologize." To her credit, her voice softened. "It's just such a shock. I didn't know her well, but she seemed nice enough." She looked around. "I take it we won't be opening today."

"No."

She nodded slowly. "Then..." She sighed and looked at Finn, her dark eyes wide. "I know you won't want to hear this, but it'll make news and you'll want to get out in front of it."

"What do you suggest? A *Facebook* post?" Aiden's voice was harsh, and he shot Kenna a disgusted look before walking off.

"I didn't mean that... oh, *shoot.*" Kenna sighed, and Finn saw the telltale glint of tears in her eyes.

"Look, ignore him, he didn't mean to snap. But, can we not think about the public relations of it all for just one day? We're all... God, *none* of us know how to deal with this. She was part of our family, you know?"

Kenna nodded and put her hand on his arm. "I do. I just feel useless, is all."

"I think we all do, right now."

Later, when the police officers had left them, the seven of them sat in the quiet restaurant. Finn decided to make them all some food ("Are we sitting shiva?" Aiden had asked, trying to lift the mood, but then shook his head, looking ashamed. "Sorry").

Finn had kissed him gently. "I guess, in a way, we are."

As he worked in the kitchen, one by one, the others came in and started to help. Even Kenna put on a chef's jacket and chopped vegetables. They worked in silence, but in a comforting way they were honoring Lisa's memory.

They sat down together in the restaurant as Aiden pulled down the shutters of the window and put the 'Closed due to Bereavement' in the window. Sarah, the hostess, arrived, tear-stained and trembling, hugging Finn hard.

"I can't believe it."

"I know."

Sarah sat down next to Jamie, taking his hand into hers and leaning her head against his for a moment. He just nodded and tried to smile.

Aiden went behind the bar and pulled out a bottle of the most expensive bourbon. He poured shots for everyone then raised his glass. "To Lisa."

They all spoke her name and drank to their dead friend. Finn tried to think of a good story to tell about Lisa, but the truth was, he had known very little about her outside work.

It was Jamie who began to speak, hesitantly, at first. "I know she seemed distant, aloof sometimes, but the truth was, she told me that when she came here, she found a family. She came from a small town in Alabama and her parents divorced when she was a kid. Her father took off, her mother turned tricks to make ends meet and feed her crack habit. Lisa even used to joke about it, sometimes, because she said it was such a god-damned cliché. The truth was, she was on her own from an early age and she learned to look out for herself. She worked three jobs even when she was underage and saved her money for cooking school. She worked her arse off and got a scholarship, finished near the top of her class. But she got a lot of shit for being a woman in the kitchen. Fucking *toxic* masculinity."

Jamie sighed and ran a hand through his dark blonde hair. "But she stuck it out, made her mark. When she saw you were opening..." He looked at Finn and Aiden. "I've told you this before and it will always be true. She *loved* working here. She told me, not long before she went missing, that this was the first time she felt as if her skills and talent were being acknowledged."

"Damn straight. She kicked ass." This was from Berto, who shifted in his chair. "Which is why..."

"None of this makes sense." Kenna spoke quietly, and they all looked at her. "I didn't know her well, but it makes no sense." She hesitated, looking around at them. "I know I shouldn't be speaking about someone I barely knew but... I can understand what it's like to find a place where you can belong for once. I understand how she felt about this place. I do."

Finn glanced at Aiden, who looked surprised at Kenna's admission. He nodded back at her. "Well, you've found a place here, Kenna." He half-smiled. "And I'm sorry for snapping at you earlier."

"It's okay. I'm sorry for my insensitive ways, I didn't mean it."

Finn sent them all home an hour later. "We'll take tomorrow off then I'll make a decision on whether we open the next day. If any of you need more time, please, tell me. It's not a problem."

He hugged Jamie. "Dude... if you need anything..."

"I guess I have to try to get in touch with her family." He sighed, running a hand through his hair, "Then... if I can't, I guess... a funeral."

"Don't worry about any of that just yet." Finn told him, gently. "We'll handle it."

Kenna didn't leave with the rest of the staff. She disappeared upstairs and Aiden and Finn went to the kitchen to clean up. Aiden gripped the back of Finn's neck and massaged it.

"You okay?"

"Not really. You?"

"Nope. This sucks."

"Yup."

They worked in silence for a time and it was only when Finn finished wiping down the steel surfaces that he noticed Aiden watching him. "What?"

Aiden smiled at him. "Lisa's story… I could see it got to you. The absent parents…"

"Mine weren't absent. Aiden. They just didn't give a shit."

"Same difference."

Finn shook his head but said nothing. When Aiden went into one of his '*let's psychoanalyze Finn*' modes, Finn tuned out. He wanted Aiden to stay clean, be honest and to love him. He didn't need a father figure. He'd been there, done that.

*And look how that turned out…*

"Man, I just want to clean up and go home, okay? It's been a day."

Aiden's face softened. "Of course, baby."

Before they left the restaurant, Finn went up to send Kenna home. "Do you need a ride? I'm worried about you working so late on your own."

Kenna shook her head. "I'm fine. The bus route goes right past my apartment. Thanks for caring."

"I'd hate anything to happen to any of my staff—" he stopped, suddenly choked. "God…"

The force of what had happened hit him suddenly, and the world shifted.

"Hey…" Kenna steered him into a chair as his breath caught and hitched in his chest. He was surprised at her strength, her slight figure easily maneuvering him. She grabbed a paper bag. "Breathe into this."

"I'm not having a panic attack, it's okay."

"Just do it."

Finn shook his head, but did as she asked. Kenna went to the door and called Aiden. "I think you should take Finn home."

Aiden took one look at Finn and nodded grimly. "Yeah… come on, lover boy. We're going home."

"I'll lock up the restaurant, don't worry." Kenna rubbed Finn's back. "Just look after yourself."

At home, Finn refused Aiden's offer of a drink. "I just want to go to bed, baby."

"Sure thing, sugar bear."

Finn smiled. "You haven't called me that for a while."

Aiden wrapped his arms around him. "Let's go to bed. I'll make you forget about today."

And he kept his word—using his lips, his tongue, his hands to make Finn's body come alive, flooding with endorphins. Finn returned his kisses, his caresses, and they made love into the early hours. It was only as they were beginning to fall asleep, that a thought came into Finn's mind.

He shook Aiden awake.

"Hey."

"Wassup?"

Finn couldn't help his grin. Aiden hated being woken up.

"Listen, it didn't occur to me earlier, but Kenna said she'd lock up the restaurant, right?"

"Mmm."

"Since when has she had a master key?"

"Dunno." Aiden turned over in bed to look at him, his eyes heavy with sleep. "But she works late, right? So, she must have a key."

"To the *back* door, yes." Finn sighed, flopping back on the pillows.

"Maybe she meant the back door?"

"Probably." Finn frowned. "I don't know why, but I think she meant the front door."

Aiden groaned. "Front door, back door, what does it matter?" He rubbed his face on his pillow. Finn looked over at him and chuckled.

"So sexy. You have drool."

"I was having a good dream when you woke me with this nonsense. Can I go back to sleep now?"

Finn moved over to kiss him, lingering over the embrace. Aiden lost the grumpy expression and smiled back. "Now you're talking."

"Oh, so you're awake now?"

"A big part of me is." Aiden leered at him and Finn chuckled.

"God, I love you, you animal."

"*Show* not *tell*, Mason." Aiden moved his body on top of Finn's and Finn ran his hands down Aiden's muscled back as their lips met again.

After Aiden had fallen asleep again, Finn lay awake staring at the ceiling, letting the endorphins that making love had sent coursing through his body relax him. It seemed incongruous, even to make love after such a sad day. Finn still couldn't get a handle on the fact that Lisa would never be at her station again, never quietly move around them as she worked, dashing them the odd shy smile. But, it seemed, they had hardly ever known her. Finn's heart ached for her sad life, feeling a kinship for the dead chef after hearing Jamie's story that he hadn't felt when Lisa was alive.

He wished he had known. He maybe could have helped Lisa get past her childhood like he had done. He could have helped her see herself for the talented, kind, sweet person she actually was, rather than the lost, lonely girl she had been carved into by her parents. Yes, he could have helped her.

He wished he had known.

# Chapter Eight

*Whitewater, Kentucky*
*Seventeen years ago…*

Finn stared out of the window, paying little attention to the teacher's monotonous drone. He had little to no interest in the American Civil War anyway, like a good fifty percent of his class, and instead, he was working out a way to make a beef daube in less than the prescribed time for his cookery class the next day. His mom would moan that he was taking up her time and using up her gas to do it at home if he risked it that evening. He had a precious hour and a quarter between the time he got home from school and when his mother got back from her job at the Dollar General in Newton. Daube usually took at least two hours, if not more, to simmer to perfection and he needed a solid B+ or A- in the class.

He'd have to risk her grouching; there was nothing else for it. He could put up with the passive-aggressive attitude for that solid B. If he didn't get his average up then he could forget about escaping Whitewater to go to cooking school after graduation, and that just wasn't an option.

The bell rang, and he gathered his books gratefully and headed out of the door. Shoving his textbooks into his locker, he didn't see the man approaching until he had slammed his door and locked it.

"Finn."

He turned to see his home economics teacher, Mr. Boyd, walking toward him. Finn relaxed. Mr. Boyd was the one tutor who understood Finn's passion for food, could get behind his laser-like focus when it came to becoming the best chef he could be.

Boyd smiled at him now. "Just checking in—I saw the recipe you submitted for the test. Ambitious."

Finn nodded. "I know, but I have to go for broke."

Boyd's smile faded a little. "Yeah… listen, have you got time for a quick chat?"

Finn chewed his lip. The truth was, if he didn't get home right now, he wouldn't have time for the daube before his mother got home.

Boyd saw his hesitation. He smiled, tipping his head to one side. "It's important."

"Sure." Hell, he'd just have to deal with his mom's displeasure. If she wanted him out of the house so desperately after graduation, then she'd have to deal with the inconvenience first.

They walked back to the kitchens in one of the outbuildings of the school. One of the few exceptional things about Whitewater High was the outbuildings they had retrofitted for cooking, shop and other classes that were considered a little less academic. The money had come from an alumnus who had made it big in the fine food world despite not having the best academic record. Lysander Ong now had three Michelin stars and a chain of high-end restaurants in Los

Angeles, Tokyo and Johannesburg, but he didn't forget his roots. He had given the graduation speech last year and Finn had sneaked into the back of the assembly hall to hear him. Ong was his inspiration, his hero, and it was because of his generosity that Finn had been able to train in this state-of-the-art campus cookery facility.

Also, Mr, Boyd was a kick-ass teacher. Boyd indicated for Finn to sit down and took a chair himself. "Okay, so… full disclosure, I've been tasked with having 'a word'." He flicked his fingers up and rolled his eyes. Finn grinned. Another reason he liked Mr. Boyd was his utter disdain for the principal, Derek Gruber, a misanthropic asshat whose idea of schooling was routed in the eighties. The *eighteen*-eighties.

"Mr. Gruber has been assessing which students are falling behind their potential. Of course, between you and me, he just means those students whose parents haven't contributed to the school… damn, me and my mouth." He grinned ruefully at Finn. "Between us, all right?"

"Of course." Finn couldn't help but snicker at his tutor's irreverence. It matched his own.

"Anyhoo, thing is, I took a look at your grades and well, I hate to admit it, but on this occasion, he might have a point. What's up, Finn? Both you and I know you are well above average in intelligence, probably the smartest kid in the school. Something going on in your personal life?"

Finn felt uncomfortable. "Not really." It wasn't a lie exactly—his parents' apathy was hardly abuse, was it?

"Hmm." Boyd nodded slowly, obviously not buying it for a second. "You getting the support you need for… your passions?"

Finn froze a little. When he spoke again, he was very careful to keep his voice steady. "My family knows I want to be a chef. I work part-time at the diner; I cook for them at home."

"Knowing about it is very different to supporting it." Boyd paused, then nodded at Finn, expecting him to speak.

Finn sighed. "There are certain things that don't happen to people like us, like our family. We get up, we go to work or school, we say grace at the supper table, we go to our room and stay quietly. Ambition is a dirty word." He stopped. He had said way too much.

Boyd nodded thoughtfully. "I understand. It's hard to keep focus on something when the people who are supposed to champion you, *don't.*"

"Exactly."

"Trouble with that is, you're handing over your agency to them, Finn, and it's entirely up to you to take it back."

Finn was irked. "But I'm just a kid."

"You're fifteen years old. Yeah, okay, so legally you're not an adult yet, but that doesn't stop you saying that this is your passion, this is what you intend to do with your life."

"That's easy to say, but you don't know the constant passive aggressive bull I get every time I use the kitchen, or ask for money to buy ingredients."

Boyd smiled. "Suck it up, kiddo. Following your passion isn't supposed to be easy." He got up, patted Finn's shoulder. "Use this place after hours if kitchen time is what's holding you back, but somehow I don't think it is. Do me a favor though… at least strive for a B in your other classes. For me—deal?"

Finn smiled gratefully at his tutor. "Deal."

When he got home, his heart sank. His mother's car sat in the driveway and when he went inside, Linette Mason had already commandeered the kitchen. Finn knew she had done it out of spite, knowing he needed to use it. It was a game of one-upmanship that they constantly played and he was sick of it.

"Hi Mom."

"I'm using the kitchen."

"I can see." He said it mildly, not wanting an argument. Instead he went to his room, changed out of his uniform and into the clothes he always wore for cooking. He wanted to be comfortable. Grabbing his backpack, he went back to the kitchen and while his mother watched, he grabbed his ingredients for the daube from the fridge compartment he saved for his cooking things. His mom might try to sabotage his cooking time but she wouldn't dare mess with the ingredients he bought with his own money.

"Where are you taking all that? If you're going to throw it out..."

"I'm not. I'm going back to school. Mr. Boyd's given me permission to use the kitchen there." He dumped the last of the food into his bag and looked at his mother. "So, I won't be in your way."

Linette's eyes narrowed. "You home for dinner?"

"I'll grab something out." He was already halfway out of the door and he felt a certain amount of smug satisfaction. That would take the wind of his mother's sails.

Only... he hated that it was even a battle. He got on his bicycle and set off back in the direction of the school. As he turned the corner, he saw his sister's beat up Impala. She slowed and wound down the window. "You escaping?"

"Got permission to use the kitchens at school."

Hannah grinned at him, saying nothing, but offering him a fist bump, which he reciprocated. Hannah got it. She fought enough battles with his mom to understand. "Laters, dude."

"Laters."

Mr. Boyd looked up as Finn knocked at the door of the kitchens. "Oh, you need it tonight?"

"If that's okay."

"Sure."

Boyd got up and cleared the counter. Finn started to unpack his stuff, then noticed Boyd had merely moved his chair out of Finn's way and was back working on his laptop. Finn felt awkward.

Boyd sensed his scrutiny. "You okay?"

"Just not used to an audience, is all."

Boyd grinned. "Well, I have to supervise, Finn. You okay with that?"

"Sure."

"Good. Just ignore me, I won't get in your way." He smiled again. "Just do what you do."

Finn nodded and began his prep, but he had trouble ignoring the man opposite him, working quietly away on his computer. After he'd prepared his mirepoix, carrots, onion and celery that was the base of every culinary dish, he looked back up at Boyd. "You sure you don't mind spending your free time here? This daube is going to take a couple hours to cook."

Jack Boyd smiled at him, and for the first time, Finn noticed the deep moss green of his eyes and the chiseled handsomeness of his tutor's features. "No," Boyd said, gently, "No, Finn. I don't mind at all."

# Chapter Nine

*The Castro, San Francisco*
*Present day…*

Finn went up to the office to find it empty. He frowned, checking his watch. Kenna should be working and now, as he listened, he heard her voice drifting up from the alleyway. He went to the window.

"You must know you're bringing down the aesthetic of the restaurant by being here. I don't mean to be rude but I assume you could just set up camp anywhere else."

"Look, missy—" John sounded pissed, not that Finn could blame him. Finn went out of the office and down the stairs. Aiden saw his face as he passed.

"Hey, what's up?"

Finn didn't answer, just waved his hand in his hurry. There was no way Kenna was going to chase off the old man, not on Finn's watch. He went out into the alleyway. "What's going on here?"

Kenna turned towards him and, although he saw two spots of pink high on her cheeks, there was also anger in her eyes. "I'm just talking to John."

"What you're doing, Missy, is trying to clean up the streets so your damn Instafriends don't see 'the hobo' sleeping rough."

For a moment, Finn was distracted by John knowing what 'Instafriends' were, but then he snapped back to the situation. "Kenna, go inside."

"But—"

"Please. Go inside and wait for me." Finn's voice had a rare bite of ice to it and to his relief, Kenna obeyed him, brushing past him in silence. Finn waited until she had disappeared before turning to John. "John, man, I'm sorry."

"Not your fault."

"You know that wasn't coming from me, right?"

John's face softened. "I know, dude. You're a good kid. That one…" He nodded in the direction Kenna had gone. "Not so much."

"She's just young, thinks everything is an excuse for looking good."

"Hmm."

"Anyway, I'm sorry." Finn turned to go then looked back, a small smile on his face. "John… Instafriends?"

"Hey, just because I live out here, doesn't mean I don't know about these things. People throw away newspapers, magazines." John's smile faded a little. "Lisa always used to bring me copies of magazines she'd finished with. *Cosmo*, stuff like that. I learn things. Modern culture and all." He sighed. "I miss that girl."

"Me too, buddy." Finn felt the pull of sadness in his chest. They stood in silence for a moment, then John nodded.

"Lisa didn't like that girl, neither. Always saw them arguing."

"What?"

John nodded. "Saw them arguing the night before Lisa disappeared." He settled back in his makeshift bed. "Yup… something not right with that Kenna chick."

Finn went inside and went up to the office, avoiding Aiden's eye. He hated doing what he was about to do. Kenna was sitting quietly, her hands tucked into her lap, her head bowed. There was something that irritated him about her posture, but he steeled himself.

"Kenna, what the hell was that about?"

She looked up. "What?"

"John. I made it clear his presence is non-negotiable."

"Finn, you hired me to craft a specific vision for your restaurant. That is what I am doing. Having a hobo yelling at the clientele isn't going to work for us. I just…"

"John, as far as I know, has never yelled at *anyone*. Certainly not any of our customers. Kenna, this is serious. We do not own the alley; it is a public highway. John has every right to be there."

"Check the local ordinances, I don't think that's true."

Finn could feel his temper beginning to roil. "Kenna, enough now. This isn't up for debate. Don't do this again. John stays. Okay?"

Kenna's face was pinched. "Fine."

She turned in her chair and punched the keyboard of her computer angrily. Finn's hand clenched at his side. Maybe hiring her *had* been a big mistake.

"Kenna…"

She ignored him and Finn sighed. It was on the tip of his tongue to ask her about the arguments with Lisa but this wasn't the time. He could imagine her tossing her dark curly bob in a huff and flouncing out, and the image amused him so much he left the room so she wouldn't see his smile. Really, the girl was ridiculous.

He was still smiling when he went back to the kitchen. Aiden whipped his butt with a dish cloth. "What the hell was all that about?"

Finn gave him a brief rundown and Aiden sighed. "Jeez."

"Yeah."

The rest of service played out without incident, but Finn was still irked by the run-in with Kenna. When he went out to take some food to John, the man had gone from the alley and Finn felt a rush of anger. Had he made himself scarce because of Kenna?

Finn took the food back in and put it in the refrigerator, slamming it too hard. He saw Kenna pass through the kitchen and could have sworn she smirked, but he couldn't bring himself to say anything. He blew out his cheeks and then checked himself. After everything he'd been through in his life, was this really the thing to get upset about? He shook his head and smiled to himself.

He felt Aiden rub his shoulders. "What's the smile about?"

"Just thinking that with everything that's happened, getting upset about a pretentious kid is the least of my problems."

"Word, K.B. Although, you do have that meeting with the bank this afternoon."

"Aww, dang, I forgot." Finn checked his watch. "Don't suppose you wanna swap identities?"

Aiden's smile was a little strained. "Your name only on the paperwork, remember? One of my dad's conditions."

Finn sighed. "Baby…"

"It's okay, K.B. Go. You've time to go home and put on the monkey suit before the meeting. I'm going to stay here, get prepped for the evening service so that you don't have to rush back." His face softened. "Honestly, I'm kind of glad you're the one doing all that. I'm useless. Plus, I have that face."

"That face?"

"The dandy highwayman face."

Finn snorted with laughter. "The dandy highwayman?"

"You know, the cad, the bounder. Completely untrustworthy. George Sanders in *Rebecca*. Or the snake in the *Jungle Book. Trussst in meeeee.*" He whirled his eyes around at his lover who grinned.

"I get the picture." Finn kissed him full on the mouth. "Sexy."

"Untrustworthy."

"I disagree." Finn scratched Aiden's stubble with his fingertips. Aiden pressed his mouth to his and for the next few minutes, nothing else mattered. Then Aiden pushed him away with a grin.

"Go, before I break every FSA regulation there is."

"Can I take your bike?"

"Sure. Just don't wrap it and yourself around any street lights."

"Funny boy." And with a last squeeze of Aiden's butt, Finn left the restaurant.

Aiden checked his phone again. In the two hours since Finn had left, Aiden had prepared the mise-en-place for the entire kitchen and was now bored. However, it was only an hour until evening service kicked off and there was no point in going home. Instead, he went upstairs to the office.

Kenna was sitting at her desk, but instead of her usual default of being on social media, she was bent over, her head in her hands. Aiden frowned. Was she crying?

Her petite shoulders were shaking. Aiden cleared his throat softly, and she started. Her face was damp with tears.

"Hey," he said, feeling awkward, "you okay?" He didn't do female tears well.

Kenna nodded, blowing her nose loudly. "I fucked up."

"What do you mean?"

She sighed. "I mean, I think Finn's going to fire me."

Aiden blinked. "What?"

She looked up at him, her dark eyes huge in her tiny face. A fleeting image of a Manga cartoon floated through Aiden's mind but he pushed it away. The girl was obviously upset.

He pulled up a chair next to her. "Talk to me."

She took her time wiping her face on her lace handkerchief. "I misspoke to John outside and Finn took it the wrong way." She sniffled. "He… yelled at me."

That didn't sound like Finn but Aiden let it slide. "Why?"

"Because I'm trying to give this place the best shot at becoming the number one place on The Castro." Her voice was rising and Aiden raised his hand.

"Okay, Kenna, breathe. Look, when it comes to John, Finn is resolute and I have to say, so are the rest of us. He's a good man, down on his luck and it's not our place to judge. Heck, Kenna, this is The Castro… it's supposed to be inclusive of everyone."

He realized he sounded preachy and when he saw her lip quivering again, he shook his head. "Sorry. But, look, Finn knows you're doing your best, and you've definitely made a difference to our social media presence. But there's more to this place than aesthetics."

She nodded. "I know. I'm learning. I… I just don't have anyone to talk to about it. You guys are always so busy in the restaurant and when I try to talk to Finn about this, I always seem to get on his wrong side." She took a deep breath in. "Please, don't tell him about this. I don't want to cause a bad atmosphere between us."

"Of course not. Just between us, okay? And you can always talk to me, you know. After service? Just come down to the kitchen and get me." He grinned at her. "Anything to get out of clean up."

She gave him a small smile then. "Thanks, Aiden."

"No problem, kiddo." He looked out of the window. "The thing with Finn is… he cares about anyone who is… let's just say, out of the normal social circles. That's simplifying it but, you should know, Finn's been through some shit in his life. It changed him, his outlook."

"What kind of things?"

Aiden shook his head. "Not my story to tell. I'm just saying, remember that Finn will fight for anyone that feels sidelined."

"Except for me."

"Do you feel sidelined?"

She shrugged. "Sometimes. I'm the only one who doesn't get involved with the kitchen, the running of the place. You're all such a team and I'm… up here."

Aiden felt uncomfortable again. "Well, we'll just have to see what we can do about that. Yeah?"

She smiled at him, a genuine smile this time. "Yeah."

Aiden got up. "Good. Now, I do have to go down, get ready for service. You'll be okay up here?"

She nodded but as he reached the door, she called him back. "Aiden?"

"Yeah?"

Her eyes met his and something burned behind them that he couldn't read. "Thank you."

He nodded, smiled and went back downstairs.

# CHAPTER TEN

Something was breaking through Finn's sleep but he kept pushing it away until, annoyed, he opened his eyes. A buzzing. His cell phone on the nightstand. He pushed it onto the floor and rolled over, nestling into the warmth of Aiden's back. He slid his arm around his lover's waist and Aiden stirred, clasping Finn's hand over his heart. Finn kissed his shoulder blade and breathed deeply, hoping sleep would take him again.

He could tell it was way too early to get up—the crack in the drapes showed the dark night outside. He rested his cheek against Aiden's cool, smooth skin. The phone buzzed against the rug, muted, but still insistent.

"Fuck's sake, answer it, for the love of God."

Finn chuckled at Aiden's gruff annoyance, but he rolled over and retrieved his phone. "Grumpy old man."

"Fuck off."

Finn snorted with laughter then answered the call. "Yeah?"

"Finn Mason?"

A voice he didn't recognize. He sat up. "Yes, this is he." He glanced over at the clock. Three thirty-seven a.m. "Who is this?"

"This is Captain Roberts with the San Francisco Fire Department. Sir, you own the restaurant named *Homefires*?"

"I do." Finn was alert now, and he shook an annoyed Aiden awake. "Is there a problem, Captain…"

"Sir, there's been a serious fire in the alley next to your restaurant and I'm sorry to report there's been a fatality. Your restaurant has some smoke damage, but the fire was contained outside. I'm asking if you could come to the location and talk with us and perhaps help with the investigation. I know it's early."

"No, no, of course, we'll come straight away." His throat felt tight, constrict, his blood cold in his veins. Fire.

*Fire.*

And a body. In his heart he knew. John.

He said goodbye to the fire chief and told Aiden in a flat voice what had happened. How he got dressed, out of the house and onto the back of Aiden's bike, he couldn't recall. Aiden held his hand after they parked the bike and walked to the waiting emergency service crews.

"Mr. Mason?"

The tall, African-American fire chief introduced himself. "Olly Roberts. I'm so sorry about this."

"Who's the victim?"

"We're not sure. He didn't have identification on him." Roberts looked sympathetically at him. "Mr. Mason, are you up to identifying the body?"

"I can try." But Finn felt as if the earth was shifting under his feet. The stench of the smoke filled his lungs, and he choked. Roberts noticed.

"Hey… hey, you okay?"

He and Aiden helped Finn sit down. Aiden looked at Chief Roberts. "He has a phobia of fire. Ironic, I know, for a chef, but…" He sighed. "We had a homeless man living outside the restaurant. John. He was a good man. If it's anyone…"

"How did he die?"

Aiden frowned at Finn's question, glancing at Roberts, who cleared his throat. "Obviously we can't say for sure, but it's not uncommon for… if alcohol or an alcoholic substitute I spilled on clothes, a cigarette…"

"John didn't smoke."

Aiden shared another glance with the Chief. "Honey?"

"He didn't smoke. He drank, yes, when he could get it, but he never smoked. Never had. He told me."

"Well, maybe something else… look, we won't know until the investigation, Mr. Mason."

Finn felt numb. "Can I see him? Has he already been taken away?"

"Not yet. We wanted to get a preliminary I.D. if we could. He's on a gurney. Over there."

"Okay. Okay."

He got to his feet, flanked by Aiden and the Chief. "I'm okay. I want to do this."

On the gurney, a black body bag. At the Chief's nod, the medical examiner unzipped the bag and pulled it apart a little. Finn looked down at John's pale face. One side of it was red raw, the flesh pulled back from his mouth in a horrific grimace.

"How come only one side of his face is burned?"

"We think he was sleeping."

"Then he couldn't have been smoking, could he?"

Finn felt grief, anger, and he looked up into Roberts' handsome face. "Could he?"

Roberts' face was impassive. "Mr. Mason, is this the man known to you as John?"

Finn nodded, then cleared his throat. "Yes. Yes, it is."

Roberts put a hand on his arm. "Thank you. It helps to know that even if he had no I.D. We can help trace his family, and, hopefully, give him a proper burial."

Finn looked up at the Chief. "If you can't find his family, I... we... want to pay for his funeral." He glanced at Aiden, who nodded.

"We do. And anything we can do to help with the investigation..." He gave Roberts their details.

"They may need to take a statement at the police station."

"Of course."

Roberts shifted his focus back to Finn. "You okay, sir?"

"I'm fine."

Finn walked slowly back to the restaurant and let them in. There was no damage that they could see but the smell of smoke permeated the kitchens and dining room.

"No point trying to air it out until the smoke from outside clears," Aiden said. Finn sat down, rubbing his hands through his hair. Aiden made them both some strong coffee and brought it to them.

He bent his head to kiss the top of Finn's. "Hey. Are you okay?"

Finn shook his head. "He didn't deserve that death, Aiden. He didn't."

"I know, Boo." Aiden stroked his lover's face and Finn leaned into his touch. He closed his eyes. So many images were coming back to him, every one of his senses heightened by the horror of the fire.

This one... and the one from before. He shuddered. He remembered the choking fumes, the weight of the body on top of him, whispering in his ear.

*I'm doing it for us...*

The dark spots dancing in his vision as the smoke filled his lungs. Unable to scream, the lack of oxygen constricting his muscles, he couldn't fight, couldn't breathe...

*Dying...*

"Finn?"

He opened his eyes to see Aiden's face, his brows knitted. "Finn... come back to me. You're here, you're safe. You are in our restaurant, you're not in that motel room."

Finn nodded, his eyes feeling heavy and tired. "I know. I know, honey. This isn't about me."

Aiden nodded but swept a hand over Finn's hair. "We'll tell the others when they get here, then go down, give our statement. If you want, we can close for the night."

"No. I want things as normal as possible. What with Lisa, and now this... *Jesus*, Aiden, what the hell?"

"Lisa was depressed, and John... I'm one hundred percent positive it was a terrible accident."

"How can you be so sure?"

Aiden shrugged. "Because what else could it be?"

Finn stared at him for a long moment, saying nothing. Aiden sighed. "No. Nope. *Not* going down that rabbit hole with you."

"Someone started that fire."

"Why, though? Who would want to kill John? He was practically a legend on The Castro. Even if some homophobic pricks… well, then, okay, yeah maybe. The police will find out. There're live cams trained on every part of this street. But I just, I think it's unlikely."

Finn stared at him some more. A thought was festering in his brain and he couldn't shake it and now he looked away. Aiden wasn't fooled. "You have some other idea?"

"It's a little coincidental, is all."

"What is?"

Finn chewed his lip. "She wanted him gone."

Aiden stared at him for a long moment then stood. "No. *No.* Are you fucking *kidding* me with this?"

"She wanted him gone."

"Think about what you are saying, Finn. Jesus, I…" Aiden broke off, and Finn could see he was furious. "No. No, you are not going to put this on that girl. She's annoying, yes, but she's not a killer."

"She argued with Lisa. Right before Lisa died. John told me."

"So? You think that tiny slip of a girl hauled Lisa to the Golden Gate and hoisted her over? Come on, man, you sound crazy."

"I have some experience in crazy, remember?"

"Yeah and now you judge everyone by that bastard's standards. Jeesh." Aiden swept a hand down his chin. "Fuck, man. You're still stuck in that motel room. You always have been."

"No, I'm not. I am more aware of people's motives, is all."

"Like I said, you judge everyone. Give them motivations that just aren't there. *Jesus.* She said you hated her and now I'm beginning to think she was right."

"Kenna said I hated her?"

"Yup. I thought she was being paranoid. Guess not."

"You two often have these intimate chats?" Finn couldn't help the note of jealousy that crept into his voice.

Aiden shot him a disgusted look. "Grow up." He stalked out of the room, Finn staring after him.

*Shit.*

Service that night was subdued and Finn was kept busy so he couldn't talk to Aiden again. Kenna showed up as usual and disappeared upstairs, and when Finn saw Aiden go upstairs, he gritted his teeth but said nothing.

When Aiden came down, his eyes were cold. "I told Kenna what happened. She's very upset."

"Really?"

"Jesus, Finn."

Finn held up his hands. "I meant nothing by that." A lie, but he didn't want to argue in front of the others in the kitchen. They had already sensed the tension between the owners.

Aiden just shook his head and went back to his station. The evening limped on and finally, when the restaurant had closed and everyone else had gone home, Finn went upstairs. As always Kenna was still in her office but as Finn entered, he saw her staring out of the window, lost in her thoughts.

"Hey."

She started and turned, blinked, and for a second in her eyes, Finn saw something other than the cool, collected emotions she usually portrayed. *Vulnerability.*

"Just wanted to say it's late. Maybe you should go home."

Kenna stared at him for a long moment and then shook her head. "No, I… No. I'm fine here."

Finn frowned. "It's almost midnight."

She met his gaze then. "I can't go home, Finn. I can't. I'd rather stay here, work through the night." She nodded to a hold-all in the corner of the room. "I'll be fine."

"You can't sleep here, Kenna…" Finn was appalled. "If you need…" He sighed. "If you need some place to stay for a few days, why not get a motel? Or stay with a friend?"

As soon as the words were out of his mouth, he regretted it. Kenna broke eye contact and looked away. *She doesn't have any friends…*

Finn rubbed his head. Was he really about to say what he was going to say? "Look…"

His cell phone ringing interrupted him and when he saw the caller ID., his eyes widened and every other thought fled from his mind. "Excuse me, Kenna…"

He stepped out of the room and answered the phone. "Hannah?"

He heard his sister chuckle. "Don't sound so surprised."

"Is everything okay? Are you alright?" Hannah never called him. *Ever*. If he was lucky, he'd get a text message once a month, an email every six. It wasn't that Hannah ignored him, she was just busy with her own life and Finn understood that. They had never been the type of siblings to sit down and chat about their feelings or feel the need to spend a lot of time together.

"Kinda. Well, no. Finn, Mom's sick."

Finn felt a ribbon of ice curl inside him. "Sick? Define sick?"

Hannah sighed. "The docs think it's lymphoma, but they're not exactly sure. But she's in a hospital in Topeka." There was a silence. "Can you come?"

Finn closed his eyes. He hadn't been back to Kansas since… since. He thought of seeing his parents again, seeing the judgement in their eyes, and the disconnect… "Of course, I can come. Are you there already?"

"Flying in tomorrow." Hannah gave a heavy sigh, which made Finn feel a little better. She didn't want to go back any more than he did. "Listen, can we meet up before going to the hospital?"

"Yes." Finn breathed out, his relief palpable. "Of course. When's your flight?"

She told him and Finn promised to call her back when he'd booked a flight. He went down to the kitchen and told Aiden. Aiden's eyes softened, their argument forgotten.

"You want me to come with you?"

Finn smiled at his lover. "No, baby, but thank you. I don't… I'm not staying long. I just can't." He blew out his cheeks. "I can't imagine Mom will want me around for long as it is and if she's really sick…"

"Yeah." Aiden came to him, wrapped his arms around him. "I know. Listen, just remember, your life is here now – and nothing, nothing, can take that away from you. Certainly not them. Hannah will have your back, right?"

Finn smiled. "It's not about me, babe. Family is still family no matter how shittily they've treated me, and Mother… *Mom*… is sick."

Aiden swept his fingers through Finn's dark hair. "Let's go home now, then, book your flight, get you packed. The sooner you go…"

He kissed Finn's mouth then, tender, soft. "I'll miss you, K.B. But I'll be here when you get back. Remember that."

It wasn't until later when Finn had finished packing that he remembered Kenna and thought guiltily about her situation. He'd been about to offer her their guest room for a few nights but was relieved now that he hadn't. Kenna was the least of his considerations right now and the thought of her being alone with Aiden…

*Now you really are being paranoid, douchebag.* Finn shrugged to himself and lugged his full suitcase into the hallway, ready for the morning.

Aiden was already in bed, reading on his laptop, his glasses sliding down his nose. He looked up and smiled as Finn slid into bed beside him. "All set?"

"Yep." Finn leaned over and kissed him. "Listen… I'm sorry about before. This morning. It was dumb of me to think Kenna would have something to do with John's death. I was just…"

"I know." Aiden stroked a finger down Finn's face. "With your history, it's understandable, if a little out there. I can hardly see Kenna as a mass murderer."

Finn snorted. "Man, my flights of fantasy…" But his voice trailed off, and he shrugged. "Hell, let's forget it. I hope to God they find John's family."

"If not, we'll make sure he gets a good funeral, a good send-off. Not like we can't afford it." He pushed the laptop over to Finn.

Finn saw the open finance database, his eyes going to the figure at the bottom of the screen. "Wow. Seriously?"

Aiden grinned. "*Homefires* is a success, K.B. You did it."

"*We* did it." Finn couldn't stop looking at the profit margin. "Holy crap."

"Well, being realistic, after word got out, we had expected an increase in looky-loos, curious about the new kids on the block, but we seem to have maintained a pretty steady clientele." Aiden paused. "I know you have issues with her, but Kenna... she's done exactly what we asked of her. She got us noticed, and your food, *your* food, Finn, is what kept people talking."

Finn grinned at his lover. "Silver tongue."

Aiden laughed. "I'm right and you know it. Now, you tired? Or am I going to get some good lovin' before you leave me, Kansas Boy?"

He'd hardly said the words before Finn rolled him onto his back and kissed him deeply.

In the middle of the night, though, long after Aiden had fallen asleep, sated and relaxed, Finn stayed awake, staring out of the window at the California night. He felt at home here, and knowing that tomorrow, he'd back in that place, back in Kansas... he felt sick at heart. Here he was Finn Mason, chef, restaurant owner, loved and in love.

Back in Kansas... he was that scared little kid again.

# Chapter Eleven

*Motel 6 just outside Whitewater, Kentucky*
*Fourteen years ago…*

Outside the motel window, Finn could hear the relentless pounding of rain and the scent of it on the dirty asphalt outside was drifting through the open window. He lay on his stomach, a myriad of emotions flooding through him.

A neon sign advertising the motel was blinking in a discordant pattern, casting a sickly yellow and orange glow in the darkened motel room. Finn started as soft lips were pressed to the small of his back and then trailed up his spine.

"Your skin tastes of salt and peaches." His lover's voice was close to Finn's ear, and he felt teeth nibbling at the lobe.

Finn was pretty sure his skin tasted of sweat and semen, but he'd taken the compliment. He rolled onto his back and gazed up at the man above him. Jack Boyd was no longer his tutor at school, but there was no way Finn was going to tell anyone about the two of them, anyway. This was too exhilarating to be anything but clandestine. He still remembered the first time Boyd had kissed him.

They'd met up after graduation, by accident Finn had thought at first, when Jack came to his diner. Finn was finishing up a double shift but seeing Jack there, he'd sat down with his former teacher to catch up.

He had thanked Boyd for kicking his butt when it came to his studies. "Thanks to you, Mr. Boyd, I get to pursue my chosen career."

"Jeez, Finn, you did that. I just gave you a little push and, by the way, I'm not your teacher any more. Call me Jack."

It hadn't been one of those 'suddenly their eyes met… and held' things, Finn thought afterwards, more of a gradual acceptance that they would share coffee every couple of days and talk about anything and everything. Jack told Finn that he was getting tired of teaching, but that Finn had inspired him to rediscover his own love of food and cookery.

"I spent three years teaching in Seoul back when I was only a little older than you, and the food, man, it was an adventure, and a revelation. I was just this kid from a small town in Washington and I was trying things I had never heard of, even in the books I'd studied or the T.V. shows." His face was lit up as he described some of the food and techniques he'd learned and Finn, having never been out of Whitewater, even for a vacation, was transported to South Korea as he listened to his friend.

Their conversations began to change into Finn making plans to travel to hone his craft, then slowly, over a few months, his plans became *their* plans.

It was October when Jack kissed him for the first time and by that time, it had seemed inevitable. They were in line at a movie house, and it just happened. He was mid-sentence and Jack leaned over and brushed his lips against Finn's. Quick. Soft. Then Jack started talking about the movie and Finn was left in confusion. In the theatre, Jack's hand was tantalisingly close to his the whole time, but Finn couldn't work out whether he wanted him to hold it, or...

His confusion was compounded at the end of the evening when Jack dropped him off at the corner of his block. Jack had called him back after Finn had gotten out of the car.

"Hey, Mason?"

Finn turned to see Jack grinning at him but there was a little doubt in his eyes. "Yeah?"

"Your move." Jack smiled and then he was gone. Finn watched his tail lights disappear.

*Your move...*

Now, a month later, with a late November rainstorm breaking over the Motel 6, Finn looked up at his lover. Finn had spent a sleepless night after that first kiss but in the morning, sitting around the breakfast table with his distant, distracted family, the decision had been clear. Jack was freedom. Jack was love.

Finn turned eighteen three days later, and it was that day, his birthday when he saw Jack again. He sent him a text message, asking to meet in a coffeehouse on Main Street and when Jack walked in, Finn got up and kissed him back, right there in the middle of the café. It was the last time they were so indiscreet.

Jack had found this motel, just outside of town where they could be together. Whitewater was far too dangerous for one of its high school teachers to be seen with a student, even an ex-student and even now, small towns bred small minds.

But this was their haven, this cheap but clean motel out on the Interstate. The first time had been just to talk, to kiss, to hold each other. To declare their mutual attraction. They made more plans, began to seriously discuss travelling together.

On the third date, Jack took Finn's virginity and Finn, all of eighteen, thought he was in love. Now, a month later, he was still in that first rush of bewildered delight.

Jack nuzzled his nose to Finn's then his mouth found his lips hungrily. After a moment, breathless, Finn pulled away, touching his fingertips to Jack's face, still not believing they had found each other.

"Is this forever?" The question sounded so cheeseball to his own ears and Finn felt his face flame but Jack's smile was kind, loving.

"I'll never let you go now, my love… not ever…"

# Chapter Twelve

*Topeka Regional Airport, Kansas*
*Present Day*

Finn saw his sister waiting for him as soon as he passed from baggage claim through to the arrivals lounge. A rush of both relief and love flooded through him. Hannah had been the only one in his family that had been of any support to him. Now, to see her looking thin and drawn, and as obviously nervous about being back home as he was, he realized he had underestimated his sister's experience of their upbringing. He had been too focused on his own misery and Hannah, stoic as always, had seemed untouchable, unflappable.

Hannah enveloped him in a bear hug—again, way, *way* out of character.

"Hey, little brother."

"Hey, sis."

They hugged for a long time and Finn could feel her body trembling. "Are you okay?"

Hannah shook her head and Finn sighed. "I know. I keep

thinking that I should only be worried about Mom, but…"

"But." Hannah nodded. "Come on. I rented a hire car so we could have some privacy to talk on the way to the hospital." She tucked a dark strand of hair behind her ear. She looked thin, and there were dark violet shadows under her eyes.

They got into the hire car and Hannah pulled out of the parking lot, joining the highway into the center of the city. "I booked us a hotel room—hope you don't mind sharing."

"Not at all. Thanks for doing that."

"No worries." She passed a hand over her eyes and the car swerved a little. "Sorry. I haven't slept for a couple of days." She gave a short laugh. "Hell, let's just call this what it is. It's hell to be back here."

Finn laughed. "Yup. So, let's pretend we're *not* here. How's New York?"

Hannah's expression softened. "It's hard work – endlessly long days and stress – and I *love* every moment." She looked over at him. "Word is, I might make editor in the next couple of years."

"That's wonderful, Han, seriously. So proud of you."

Hannah gave her first genuine smile. "Thanks. Talking of proud… I've been keeping up with the San Francisco restaurant news. You're getting to be a big deal, bro. Nothing less than what you deserve."

"You keep up with West Coast news?" Finn grinned at his sister. "I thought the world ended at the Hudson for you Noo Yoik peeps."

"Ha ha!" Hannah chuckled softly, then looked over at him. "We did it, you know. We got away."

"And now we're back."

"Which just shows the kind of people we are." A note of anger was in her voice now. "*We* grew up even if *they* never did. We're good people, Finn. They don't and never did deserve us."

They drove in silence for a while, both lost in their own thoughts. Finn considered if what Hannah said was true, especially as lately, he'd felt more anger than he had since that terrible day in the Motel 6 all those years ago. That anger made him uncomfortable.

"Hannah, can I ask you something?"

"Of course."

Finn hesitated. "Ever get a feeling about someone that you can't shake? Like they're somehow… god, I don't even know. There's this girl, Kenna… she handles our social media presence, and she's doing a great job. It's just…"

"Just what?"

Finn chewed his bottom lip. "Since we've known her, there's been a couple of things, pretty serious things, that have happened. One of our chefs killed herself. And a homeless guy, John, he was killed in a fire in the alleyway behind the restaurant a couple of days ago."

"And they connect to this girl, how?"

Finn felt a little foolish. "On the surface… they don't. So, yeah, Lisa—the chef who died—didn't like Kenna, and a couple days before the fire, John had an argument with her, but…"

"A stretch to think she was involved?"

"Yes and yet…"

Hannah suddenly turned into the parking lot of the hotel and stopped the car. "This is the place." She switched off the ignition and turned to face her brother. "So, you got a gut feeling or what?"

"I have. I truly have, but I have no reason for it, and Aiden thinks it's because of what happened between me and Boyd, that it's coloured my reaction."

"Has it?"

"Probably. Why wouldn't it?"

Hannah studied him. "Even so, you should go with your gut, bro. You're not a kid any more, and I always think instinct is an under-used human sense." She looked out of the window. "Like when Dad called, telling me about Mom. I got this… I think this is it, Finn. I think she's dying and Dad is in denial but he called me… us… so we could say goodbye. That's what my gut is telling me."

"Dad *called* you."

Hannah smiled gently at him. "He asked me if I knew where you were, asked if I could get in touch. Believe it or not, he wants you there."

"Right."

"Seriously. He sounded broken, Finn and we both know what that's like." She sighed and shook her head. "Sorry, went off on a tangent. This girl…"

"It's okay. Let's get this visit done, see Mom and…" Finn trailed off. "God, I have had enough of death lately."

"Well, if, like they say, it comes in threes… sorry, morgue humor. It helps." Hannah grimaced slightly. "Come on. Let's check in and then we can do this thing."

Acute myeloid leukaemia, not lymphoma. Finn's dad had misunderstood. Linette Mason had a poor prognosis, and although the oncologist was very patient and explained everything, all Finn heard was that his mother had less than a fifteen percent chance of surviving five years. Linette herself seemed strangely sanguine, resigned, but Finn's father, Duke, was shattered. It was unsettling to see him like that—Finn, who had never been close to either of his parents—had always thought of Duke as a big bear of a man, looming over them all, but now he seemed shrunken, diminished by grief. He held Linette's hand tightly—something Finn and Hannah had never seen him do.

Finn leaned over and kissed his mother's cool cheek. "Hello Mother."

Linette gave him a weak but genuine smile. "Finn, baby, would you please call me Mom? Mother makes me sound dead already."

Finn winced but forced a smile. "Of course. Hi, Mom. Dad." He put his hand on his father's shoulder and Duke patted it absent-mindedly.

"Hey, kid." Duke looked at Hannah, blinked as if seeing her for the first time. "Hannie."

"Hey. Pa."

Linette chuckled. "Weird time for a family reunion." She focused on Finn. "You look good, son. Healthy. Happy."

"I am, both. But how are you feeling, Mom?"

"Oh, you know. Cancer-y." She rolled her eyes. "That was a joke. Listen, the only way I'm getting through this is making funnies so at least give me a pity laugh."

Who *was* this woman? She bore no resemblance to the woman who had thrown Finn out of her house fourteen years ago. No resemblance to the woman who refused to visit him in the hospital after...

Linette slipped her free hand into Finn's. "Hannah tells me your restaurant is doing well. How's your boyfriend… Adam?"

"Aiden." Finn shot a look at his sister who was staring out of the window, avoiding his gaze. "He's good. The restaurant is doing well, thank you."

He felt awkward and lapsed into silence as Hannah, seeing his discomfort, took over the conversation. Linette kept her hand clasped onto Finn's until her eyelids flickered shut and it slipped to the bed. Duke rallied. "Listen, kids, she'll be asleep for a while and you've both had long journeys. You should go back to your hotel, get some rest."

"What about you, Dad?"

Duke smiled at his daughter. "I'm okay, Hannie. Really. I'll go down to the cafeteria, grab some supper." He glanced at Finn. "Bet it won't be as good as your food, son. Maybe you could…"

"I'd love to," Finn said, with feeling. "I'd love to cook for you and Mom."

Duke cleared his throat, embarrassed by the sudden emotion in the room. "Okay then. You two get along now."

Hannah wanted to catch up on work, so Finn snagged his cell phone and went outside into the hotel courtyard to call Aiden. "Hey, Boo."

"Hey, K.B. How's Kansas?"

"You know. Mom's pretty sick, Dad's… god, I don't even recognize him." Finn filled Aiden in on everything, then asked about the restaurant.

Aiden chuckled. "It's fine, babe. We miss you but we can manage for a couple of days. Listen, we had an influx of bookings, so much so we had a waitlist. Kenna's been working magic again, even from her sick bed."

"Sick bed?"

"Yeah she called in earlier. She has stomach flu or something, so I told her to stay home." Aiden sighed. "God, it's weird not having you here."

Finn felt better, then, and after chatting for a while, he said goodbye to Aiden and ended the call.

It was late afternoon, the sun dipping below the horizon, casting an orange glow and Finn decided to walk around the local area for a while, give Hannah more time to work.

As dusk fell, he found himself on 10th and Jackson, and saw the magnificent Kansas State Capitol building, the spotlights on the domed roof illuminating the majesty of it. He stopped for a moment and considered it. He'd been to Topeka before, only once or twice but had never really considered it to be somewhere he could sightsee. Hell, it was just Topeka, but now, looking at this glorious building, the seat of both executive and legislative branches of government for the state, he felt like he had missed out.

It had never felt like home, Kansas, not like San Francisco. He had never felt a kinship with the place but now, having sated his eyes on all California's wild beauty, he could see what he had ignored as a younger man. Topeka might not be a hotbed of excitement, but it was still a lovely place. Finn chuckled and shook his head. Maybe so, but it would never be home. It still felt strange to be here.

Finn walked back to the hotel, and it wasn't until he had almost reached it when his spidey senses tingled. Someone was following him; he was sure of it. The sidewalks weren't exactly packed with people and he could hear the echo of footsteps that were not his own behind him.

He stopped, feigning an interest in a store's window display, hoping that he was just being paranoid, but the footsteps stopped too. *Fuck.* He shot an annoyed glance behind him, expecting to see a guy or a bunch of guys waiting to mug him. Yeah, this might not be New York or 'Frisco but…

He saw a small figure, turning away from him and crossing the street. He—or she—was petite and was walking quickly over to the other side of the street where Finn saw someone else in shadow. The first person walked up to them and together they turned and strolled away down the street. Finn stared after them. There was something familiar about their gaits but from here, he couldn't see their faces, or even determine their genders.

He sighed. *Whatever.* They obviously had nothing to do with him, right? Finn went back to the room to find Hannah had ordered them room service and was making her way down a bottle of wine. She nodded to the tray of food. "It's still hot. Just burgers and fries but they're good."

Finn ate while Hannah flicked through the channels on the television. She settled on some reruns of *Friends*, then turned the volume down. "So."

"So what?"

"Tell me more about this Kenna girl. I went online earlier, just to check out your website, what she'd done."

"Impressed?"

Hannah nodded, but Finn saw hesitation in her eyes. "What?"

"It's just… you sure that's all her own work?"

Finn frowned. "What do you mean?"

"I mean… the girl likes to co-opt other people's ideas. Does she spend all day surfing *Instagram*?"

Hannah slid her laptop over to him. On the site, Finn saw Kenna's page, the photographs she had saved from the web over a period of time and some of the images she had taken at Homefires. At first, Finn couldn't see what Hannah was referring to, but then as he scrolled down, he saw it. He shrugged. "Hey, listen, we all have to get inspiration for somewhere."

"Oh, I agree," Hannah said, "but when does inspiration become appropriation? Plagiarism? If you look at the comments under her posts, I mean her *actual* photographs of *Homefires,* there's an awful lot of people calling her out. And she claps back too, look…"

Hannah scrolled down the page and pointed out a selection of text to Finn.

| | |
|---|---|
| *Benkhampshire* | **Hey *KennaHomefiresSF*, are you ever going to credit CaitlynSee for the design of this photo? It's practically an identical copy of the aesthetics of the work she submitted last year.** |
| *KennaHomefiresSF* | **Thanks for your feedback, *Benkhamphire*, but this was an original concept I came up with at the beginning of the *Homefires* campaign.** |
| *Benkhampshire* | **Riiiiiiight. So, it's just coincidental then? *Sure*, Jan.** |
| *KennaHomefiresSF* | **Slander is still a criminal offense, right, *Benkhampshire*?** |
| *Benkhampshire* | **Slander is spoken defamation, not written down. That's libel. And it's not libellous if it's provable. Just take a look at when Caitlyn—who, by the way, could run rings around you—posted her work. It isn't just me saying this. I know you've been deleting comments.** |

*KennaHomefiresSF* **I haven't been deleting jacksh*t and I would ask you to refrain from 'libelling' me and my restaurant, then, a$$hole.**

"Oh, you are freaking *kidding* me?" Finn shook his head, disgusted. "Is she for real?"

"Well," Hannah stuck her tongue in her cheek, "it is *her* restaurant, after all. But seriously, this isn't professional, bro, and it could damage your business."

"Fuck."

"Sorry."

Finn sighed, running his hand through his hair. "No, it's good you found this out. Aiden and I, we kinda left Kenna to do her thing, but it looks like we should have managed her a little more. *Jeez…*"

"Don't stress, bro. Look, I've been thinking about what you said about gut instinct. When we leave here, I'm coming back to San Francisco with you for a few days."

Finn was surprised. "You are?"

Hannah grinned. "Yeah, I've been thinking about it for a while now. I took a couple of weeks off just in case… you know. I'm going to come back with you and check this chick out. Something's hinky about her."

Finn felt both elated that Hannah would see his success in person, and relieved that she too thought something was up with Kenna Mitchell. "I would like that."

Hannah closed the laptop. "Wanna watch *Friends* with me? Eat and drink our way through the mini-bar?"

Finn laughed and nodded. "Hell, yes I do. Let's get trashed and cuss out Ross."

"Word, bro, word."

"Loser."

"Jerk."

Finn laughed and, grabbing one of the tiny bottles of vodka from the mini bar, scooched down next to his sister to relax for the evening.

He didn't know when he fell asleep, but he woke when Hannah's cell phone rang just past six the next morning to hear their father informing them their mother had died.

# Chapter Thirteen

*San Francisco,*
*Present day…*

"I should be there. I should come out to Kansas, be with you." Aiden balanced the phone between his shoulder and his jaw as he struggled to unlock the door. "God damn, what the hell is wrong with this lock?"

Finn, on the other end of the line, gave a tired chuckle. "Call a locksmith. And, no, babe, don't come. Dad doesn't want anyone but immediate family there. We're not even holding a wake. He's in major denial."

"What about you?" Aiden looked up as the door opened from inside and Kenna smiled at him. Aiden smiled a hello, pointing unnecessarily to the phone in his hand. Kenna nodded and went back upstairs. "What do you need?"

"I need to get this over with and come home to you. I offered to stay, help Dad out, but he wants to be alone. Honestly, I'm torn, but he's insistent."

Aiden sighed. "I hate to say it but you just got to let him do what he needs. If he needs to be alone…"

"Yeah. Listen, Hannah is still coming back with me." Finn was quiet for a while and when he spoke again, his voice quivered. "I honestly never expected to be this upset, Aiden. It's not like we were close, although, she was… changed when I saw her in the hospital. There was a warmth there that was missing before. Shit, Aiden, why does this hurt so much?"

"Oh, baby." Aiden's heart ached for his love. "I'm so sorry."

"Yeah."

Aiden let Finn have a moment. "Listen… I haven't talked to Kenna about what you told me yet."

"Good. Don't. We'll handle it when I get home… unless she goes off on someone again, then, hell, I don't know."

"I'll keep an eye on her. I miss you, babe."

Aiden heard Finn sigh. "I miss you too. I'll be home soon."

Aiden slipped his cell phone back into his pocket and headed back into the restaurant. Dumping his bag, he opened the back door to take in a delivery, thanking the driver and signing off on the fresh food on the trays.

After shifting the trays into the walk-in freezer, Aiden went upstairs. As he walked to the bathroom, he heard an odd noise coming from the office and stuck his head inside. To his dismay, he saw Kenna wiping tears away from her face. "Hey, hey, hey, what's up? You okay?"

Kenna looked embarrassed. "Sorry, I'm fine."

Aiden put down the stack of towels he was holding. "You're obviously not. What is it?" He glanced at the open laptop in front of her. "Kenna… has someone upset you?"

"No, not really. It's probably me being paranoid, but..." She indicated the computer and Aiden squinted at the screen.

Under one of her Instagram posts – an innocuous collage of images from the restaurant and a reminder of opening times – Aiden saw Finn had commented, appearing to apologize for something Kenna had written.

| | |
|---|---|
| *HomeFires:* | **Hey there! I'm sorry for the above comment—please note that *KennaHomeFiresSF* does not speak for the restaurant on this occasion and that the above opinion is hers and not that of the restaurant or the owners. If any offense was caused, we truly apologise and we hope to see you on the Hill for one of our starters on the house.** |
| *KennaHomefiresSF:* | **We open at lunchtimes now, so come on in for some snacks and great ambiance.** |
| LolaFonsecca: | **We had a great time at HomeFires—thanks to KennaHomeFires for letting us know about this great place!** |

Aiden swept his eyes over more of the the comments above and below, but Finn's response was seemingly out of the blue and not connected to anything that either Kenna or the commenters had said.

Aiden's first thought was that maybe Kenna had deleted one of her own posts. He glanced at her. "Well, it seems unusual. Perhaps Finn misread your quote, or maybe..." Even to his own ears, it sounded like crap. He changed tack.

"Hey, look, don't get upset. You're doing a great job of our social media presence, you know? We wouldn't be where we are without you."

Kenna sniffed. "Finn doesn't think so. I don't think he likes me much."

Aiden put a hand on her shoulder awkwardly. "Of course, he does." Something caught his eye then and, frowning, he went to the closet. A bright flash of blue fabric had caught his attention and as he opened the door, a hastily rolled up sleeping bag unraveled from the closet. For a second, he just stared at it. "What's this?" He pulled out the sleeping bag and held it up, turning to look at Kenna. Her cheeks were bright pink.

"I… I've had to sleep here for a couple of nights, is all."

Aiden gaped at her. "Why?"

Kenna sighed. "My roommate… she's a psycho. She goes through my stuff, and steals things and she… god, Aiden, it all sounds so school girlish when I say it, but I hate being there. I hate it. I stayed a couple of nights in a motel, but I can't keep doing that, and I don't have the security deposit for another place and—" Her voice was getting higher and more panicky and Aiden held up his hands.

"Woah, woah, woah, take a breath, Kenna. Breathe." Damn, he hated scenes like this; he was no good at handling them. Hell, he could hardly handle it when he freaked out himself. *No, doofus, that's why you used for years…*

Aiden shut himself up and put the sleeping bag on the desk. "Look, we can't have you living here, sleeping on the floor. You living in the office is not an option. I'm not even sure whether Health & Human Services would come down on us for it."

Kenna looked like she might burst into tears. Aiden sighed. "Come down, Kenna. I'll make you something to eat and we'll talk. Updating Facebook can wait for an hour or so."

He had hoped to get his *mise-en-place* done early today; with Finn being out, he'd had to cover both of their duties in the kitchen, but clearly, this took precedence.

As he made the coffee and flipped a grilled cheese sandwich over in the pan, he remembered what Finn had said about John's death. *She wanted him out of here.* The fleeting thought that his lover might have been right about that; if Kenna was sneaking back into *Homefires* to sleep at night, she wouldn't want John snooping and possibly snitching on her.

*Don't be an idiot. That's no reason to kill someone.* Aiden shook his head, berating himself. *Nope.* He wouldn't go down that same paranoid path that Finn had. Kenna was no killer. He plated up the grilled cheese and passed it to Kenna. "Here. Eat up." He studied her as she ate.

"So… what else has your roommate been doing?"

"Last week, I left my laptop open by accident and she'd posted some vile things in my name." Kenna put down her sandwich. "Stuff that could have affected the restaurant. I went off on her. We haven't spoken since, but she's always there. She doesn't work."

Kenna wiped her hands on her napkin and took a long drink of water. "I don't want to cause you any trouble, Aiden. I think Finn doesn't get me or I irritate him. It's just the feeling I get from him. Lately, I've been feeling like I can't please anybody." Her voice quivered and Aiden felt a surge of sympathy for her. Sitting there in her tea-dress, she was tiny and the look in her eyes was… lost. He'd seen that look before, a lot, in the eyes of the man he loved.

He sighed. "Look, maybe we can give you an advance on your paycheck so you can find a place."

She nodded but didn't say anything, just kept looking at him with those huge dark eyes. Aiden nodded to her plate. "Finish your food, Kenna. We'll figure something out."

* * *

There was something exciting about bringing Hannah back to San Francisco with him—she was the one member of Finn's family who he wanted to impress because she'd been the only one to support him.

They caught a cab back to the apartment, Finn having assured Aiden that they'd be okay to find their way home. As the cab wound its way through the San Francisco dusk, he pointed out all the obvious tourist sights, knowing Hannah was grinning at him because, as a fashion editor, she'd been there many times before.

Finn smiled ruefully. "I know you know this stuff, but you've never seen it through my eyes, sis."

"I know, I'm just teasing. Finn. I wouldn't be here if I didn't want to see the life you have built for yourself. I'm really proud, you know?"

Finn nodded, tried to smile but couldn't speak for a moment. *Proud.* That was a word he never thought he would hear from a member of his blood family, even Hannah.

The cab drove past *Homefires,* but they didn't stop. Finn was pleased that it looked alive with diners and atmosphere, and Hannah looked impressed.

"You are going to cook me something spectacular when we go there, right?"

"Hell, yes. The best."

They chatted until the cab pulled up outside Finn and Aiden's apartment. Finn lugged both their cases upstairs and opened the door. A wave of soft music flooded over him and he frowned.

"Aiden?"

He stepped aside to let Hannah in as he heard the music stop and the sound of a glass being placed on a counter top. Footsteps, but not Aiden's heavy ones. Finn frowned, then his eyes widened as Kenna came into view. She didn't look surprised to see him. "Oh, hi."

"Kenna… Where's Aiden?" He knew it was a stupid question, but he couldn't quite believe Kenna was in his apartment alone.

"Work, silly." Kenna giggled, then her eyes flicked to Hannah. "Hey there, you must be Finn's sister."

"Hi." Hannah sounded as disconcerted as Finn felt. He shook himself, setting the bags down.

"Kenna… what are you doing here?"

Her smile faltered. "Aiden… didn't tell you?"

A coil of anger was beginning to spiral inside Finn. "Obviously not."

Kenna's expression shifted to uncertainty. "Well… he said I could use your couch for a couple of nights. I had to leave my apartment… Finn, I'm sorry, Aiden told me he was going to tell you." She looked around him at Hannah. "He offered me the guest room, but I knew you were coming to stay and would need it."

"Funny," Hannah said, her tone icy, "I only just made up my mind to come."

Kenna waved her hand dismissively. "I'm sure Aiden said something… I must have misread. But you're here now."

As Finn watched, she grabbed Hannah's bag and lifted it into the guest room. "There you go. Could I offer you both some refreshment?"

Finn gaped at her, then shook his head. "No… thanks. Listen," he shot a look at Hannah, "we were just dropping the bags off. Hannah wants to see the restaurant, don't you?"

"Yup."

Kenna shrugged. "Okay. I guess I'll see you later."

Hannah nudged Finn. "Just give me a minute to freshen up."

"Sure thing."

Hannah disappeared into the guest room and closed the door. Kenna was smiling, but the smile did not reach her eyes; Finn clenched his fists. "Excuse me, Kenna."

He went into his and Aiden's room and shut the door. What the actual fuck was going on? He swept his eyes over the room. His skin itched with annoyance and a certain sense of paranoia. Why the hell hadn't Aiden told him? Moreover, why the hell hadn't Aiden asked him if it was okay for Kenna to park on their couch? He'd called Aiden from the fucking airport and not once had he said anything about… Finn hissed out a long breath. *Let him explain himself. You owe him that much.*

Out of the street, he looked at Hannah who blew out her cheeks. "So that was Kenna, huh?"

"The one." Finn started to laugh as Hannah pulled a face.

"I mean, jeez… *could I offer you both some refreshment?"* Hannah mimicked Kenna's simpering tone so perfectly that Finn busted up. Hannah shook her head. "Get over thine self, madam… and what the *fuck* was she wearing? Was she about to milk a herd of cattle? Does she have a yoke somewhere?"

Finn chuckled. "Mean, but true."

"She's Heinous Heidi, that's what she is."

They managed to flag down yet another cab—*I really need to buy a car,* Finn thought—and they went back to *Homefires.* As he opened the door, a wave of noise, chatter and laughter poured out. As he steered Hannah through the throng, he was continually stopped by the patrons, some he knew and some he didn't. He felt proud again that Hannah was seeing this, and he could tell, by the smile on her face, she was impressed with her little brother.

In the kitchen, the noise and heat ratcheted up a notch, and it was a full five minutes before Finn fought his way through to find Aiden in the freezer, leaving Hannah back in the bar.

For a moment, he stood at the door, watching his lover as he gathered ingredients for whatever dish he was about to prepare.

Aiden turned then started, cussing loudly as he saw him, then laughed. "Hey, K.B."

He put down the food and came to Finn, sliding his bag hand onto the back of Finn's neck and kissing him fiercely. "God, I missed you."

The kiss was almost worth forgiving Aiden for Kenna. Almost.

"Well, at least you weren't lonely."

Aiden, to his credit, looked guilty. "Ah, about that…"

"Yeah."

Aiden turned to pick up his ingredients. "Finn, I'm sorry, I meant to tell you, it just got crazy here. She was sleeping up in the office – can you believe that? Anyway, I tried to help out, finding her some place—and she has got a lead on something—but she needed a place to crash until then." He looked apologetically at Finn. "It's just for a few days, I swear."

"I don't mind her being there." Actually, he did, but… "It's just… you could have warned me. I did tell you Hannah was coming with me."

"I know."

"Huh."

Aiden stopped. "What?"

"Kenna made it seem as if you'd forgotten. She mentioned you offered her the guest room."

"I offered her the couch." Aiden looked annoyed now and Finn stepped aside to let him go back to his station. "Babe, what would you have done? She would have been homeless for one thing—her roommate sounds like a psycho." Aiden began to chop an onion with sharp, violent movements and gently, Finn put his hand on his lover's hand.

"Hey, stop, you'll cut yourself. It's okay." He leaned his forehead against Aiden's. "It's good to see you, Boo."

"Dudes, *gross*." The mood was broken by Berto's voice, and Finn and Aiden laughed as their co-worker and friend made a face. "You get all romantic in here and I'm out."

Berto and Clyde began their usual mockery of Finn—it was how he knew they were glad to see him back. He busted their chops for a while, then went back out to see Hannah who was surrounded by beautiful boys. She was holding her own too, much to Finn's amusement, flirting back as they bought her drinks.

The boys melted away, grinning, as Finn sat down next to his sister.

"Well, they're adorable."

Finn looked over at their table. "Regulars, almost since the beginning. I hate to admit it, but they came in after seeing Kenna's

Instagram posts."

"So, she's been an asset?" Hannah picked the olive from her drink and popped it into her mouth.

"I can't say she hasn't brought us business, that wouldn't be fair."

"But you're hesitant? Come on, Finn, this is me. Be honest, there's something about her you don't trust, right? I can see it in your face."

Finn sighed. "I cannot put my finger on it. It's just, ever since she's been around, stuff has happened and not just little stuff like the social media arguments. Lisa committed suicide. John died. The fire." He signaled to David. "Hey, dude, another round please?"

"Sure thing."

Finn turned back to Hannah. "Being serious for a second… what was your impression, earlier? Forgetting that it was a surprise she was there."

Hannah picked at the bar snacks David put down for them. "Total truth?"

"Total."

"I wasn't impressed. The whole vintage hipster thing is so contrived and wholly unoriginal nowadays. The attitude… all that simpering falseness. Yuck."

Finn snorted. Hannah had never been one to hold back. "Tell it like it is."

"Seriously, bro, I know a snake when I see one." Hannah studied him carefully. "You got anything in the apartment you wouldn't want anyone to see?"

"Like what? Porn?"

Hannah rolled her eyes. "I assume you would have that… but no.

What I mean is, anything personal… like stuff about you know who."

"Boyd?" Christ, even now to say his name was painful. "Nope. Any legal stuff I left at the lawyer's office. I didn't want any reminders."

Hannah's shoulders relaxed a bit. "Good. Because I don't trust Kenna for a second not to use something like that against you. It's a nice gesture for Aiden to let her stay, but you want some advice?"

"Always."

Hannah smirked, but there was little humor in it. "Get her out and keep her out. As soon as you can, little brother."

# Chapter Fourteen

Finn was thinking about her words later when he and Aiden were in bed. Aiden was already asleep, his thickly-muscled arm looped around Finn's chest, his shaggy head buried in the crook of his shoulder. The apartment was silent, Hannah asleep in the guest room and Kenna on the couch. She'd already been asleep when the other three had gotten home that night—at least, it *appeared* as if she was asleep.

Whether she knew it or not, Hannah had triggered something in Finn. Not that she had meant her words any other way than to help him, but all his doubts, all his paranoia about Kenna came flooding back.

Was it just him? Was he having some kind of delayed post-traumatic thing and was he focusing all of his pain from what Boyd had done to him on this silly girl? The thoughts gnawed at him over and over and it was almost light before he finally got to sleep.

In the morning, he got up to an empty bed and heard Aiden laughing with Hannah in the kitchen. He padded out, his hair sticking up everywhere and Hannah, always observant, grinned at him. "*Hawt*, bro, *hawt*."

"Hey, it's dangerous to anger the Beast before his coffee," Aiden warned her, handing Finn a huge mug of steaming coffee. "Morning, K.B."

Finn mumbled a greeting into his coffee, his gaze slipping through to the living room and the empty couch. "Where's Kenna?"

"Bathroom."

Finn grunted and sat down. Hannah ruffled his hair. "Man, you really are a grump."

"He's never been a morning person," Aiden smiled back at her, "but give it a minute until the caffeine kicks in."

"I'm fine." Finn ran a hand through his hair and smiled at them both. "You're getting on well."

"He takes care of my baby brother," Hannah said softly, "of course we're getting on."

Finn finished his coffee and went to shower, but as soon as he stepped into the en-suite bathroom in his and Aiden's room, he stopped. Kenna was there, wrapped in a barely-fitting towel and sorting through the bathroom cabinet.

"Can I help you?"

She spun around and laughed. "Oh, I'm sorry, Finn. I forgot to pack shampoo, and I heard you all talking. Didn't want to disturb."

Finn pointed silently at the bottle of shampoo on the shelf in the shower. "Oh, right, thanks." She squirted a little into her hand. "I'll buy you a new bottle, I promise."

Finn stared at her. Was this what it was going to be like? Kenna didn't move, just stared back and then slowly, but very deliberately, she let her towel fall to the bathroom floor.

Finn turned and walked out of the bathroom without comment. He went into the kitchen, filling a glass of water for something to do until he heard Kenna go back into the family bathroom and shut the door. Finn kept his face neutral but inside he was annoyed—and disturbed. What the fuck did she think she was doing?

Kenna left after she was dressed, to Finn's relief, and he, Aiden and Hannah went to Golden Gate Park to walk and catch some air. Aiden was teasing Hannah about sightseeing and she was giving it back.

"I don't care if it's cheesy, I want to do it. Tell him, Finn."

Finn realized he hadn't been listening. "Um…"

Hannah rolled her eyes. "Doofus. I want to go to Lombard Street and run down it. See if I can stop or end up in the Bay."

Aiden was grinning. "Girl, your geography is for shit."

"Jerk."

Finn smiled. *Focus on this, focus on the positive.* Hs sister and his love were both here, joking with each other, enjoying one another's company, his restaurant was a success and he was… what was he? Focusing on Kenna to assuage his guilt at being happy? Trying to find something bad that would prove him unworthy of what? *God?*

"Scary face." Hannah pointed at him as they walked, and Aiden peered at him.

"'Sup?"

Finn smiled ruefully. "Just wondering why I always lean towards snatching defeat from the jaws of victory."

"Ah." Hannah rubbed his back.

Aiden shrugged. "You are who you are, baby. After everything that happened to you back then, it's not surprising. Believe it or not, you are a million miles from the boy I met that day. The boy who literally hauled me out of the gutter."

"Hear, hear." Hannah said quietly. "Don't let that little snake get to you; she pales in comparison to what Boyd did to you."

"Yeah."

Finn felt Aiden slip his fingers between his and squeeze his hand and the three of them walked in silence for a while. They stopped at the Japanese Tea Garden and went into the teahouse for something to drink. Aiden excused himself to go to the bathroom and Hannah sipped her tea, watching her brother.

"Finn... there's something I need to talk to you about."

"Go for it."

Hannah put her cup down, hesitating. "Back in Topeka... one night when I came home from hospital, I needed some air, so I got the cab to drop me a little way from the hotel. It wasn't late, so I figured it was safe and so I was walking back and... god, Finn."

She looked sick and Finn frowned. "What is it, Han?"

She met his gaze. "I saw Jack Boyd."

The words were like a hammer blow to Finn's heart. "You're mistaken."

"No. I'm not." She leaned forward, grasping Finn's hand. "He was watching the hotel. I think... no, shit, that's crap, I *know* he knew you were there, and that's why he was there."

"But... we have the restraining order. At least in Kansas, he had to keep away from me as part of his deal."

Hannah gave him a sad smile. "What's a piece of paper going to do to stop him? Technically, he didn't go anywhere near you."

"Was there a girl with him?" Finn said suddenly. His heart was pounding hard against his ribs. When Hannah nodded, he sighed: "I saw him. He followed me and she… whoever she was… was with him. I think he was using her to see if it really was me."

"He was at Mom's funeral."

Another hammer blow. "*What*?"

"At the back when she was being buried. He saw me recognize him and took off. I could hardly run and scream after him although God knows, that's what I wanted to do." Hannah chewed her lip. "Should I not have told you?"

"No, you did the right thing." Finn saw Aiden come toward them. "But we should stop talking about it now."

Hannah followed his gaze, then smiled weakly at Aiden as he sat down. "What did I miss?"

"Not much," Finn lied smoothly. "Just explaining to my sister why Lombard Street doesn't empty into the Bay."

Aiden chortled. "You still on that?"

"Call me a doofus." Hannah shrugged, going along with the lie, much to Finn's gratitude.

Finn didn't have the opportunity to talk to Hannah privately again that day. At work, Hannah scrubbed in and helped with the menial tasks much to Finn's amusement. "Hey," she said, with a grin, "this way I can get an exclusive on kitchen fashion."

"I'm always available for modelling," Clyde said, and he struck a pose, his butt sticking out, his forefinger pressed coquettishly against his lips.

"Dear *god*," Aiden said, making a gagging noise as the kitchen busted up.

"My sister doesn't work for a porn magazine, Clyde," Finn whipped a dishcloth against his chef's butt.

Hannah was feigning being sick. "I can never, ever unsee that."

"You are *welcome*, missy," Clyde said with a big grin. The crew teased Hannah mercilessly throughout the evening service, but she took it all and gave it back with equal enjoyment.

Kenna stayed upstairs and Finn wondered if she was embarrassed about her behaviour that morning. What the hell had she been thinking? He was glad she stayed out of his sight.

* * *

It was the last day of Hannah's visit, a week later, when things started to get really weird. Just after lunch, Finn was in the office helping Hannah book a flight back to New York. Hannah was watching him when she spoke up. "Did you ever ask Kenna about those Instagram posts?"

"I haven't. Aiden told me her roommate had been posting in her name, so I didn't think it was worth pursuing." He turned to face his sister. "To be honest... I didn't want to rock the boat any more. I'm tired of worrying about it. As long as the business isn't affected..."

"But if she is copying someone else, that could have a negative impact. I'm serious. A few years ago, at the magazine, we found out one of our freelancers was plagiarising from a little-known beauty blog. We fired him but the damage to the magazine's reputation took months, hell, maybe even years to repair. You don't want any part of that, Finn. None."

"Part of what?"

They both started as Kenna came into the room. She was carrying a cup of coffee and put it onto the desk with a little too much force, splashing herself. She cussed as the hot liquid burned her fingers. Finn got up and grabbed a glass of cold water. "Here."

Kenna ignored him, just sat down at her desk and turned toward the computer.

"Have you finished with this?"

Hannah and Finn exchanged a look. "Sure."

Kenna clicked the browser shut and opened up a Word file. Hannah narrowed her eyes. "So… Kenna. I have a couple questions about your Instagram postings."

Finn sighed, but was still kind of curious where Hannah was going with this. Kenna turned her gaze to Hannah.

"Oh, do you need some help with the magazine's page? I have noticed it looking a little… *prosaic*, lately."

One-Nil to Kenna.

Hannah's eyes took on a dangerous look that Finn recognized from old. He watched in horrified fascination, knowing that riling Hannah was Kenna's biggest mistake yet. His sister wasn't nearly as soft as he was.

"No, *dear*. I'm talking about the fact that a lot of your content is awfully similar to some other influencers."

Hannah let the accusation hang in the air and for a moment, Finn wondered if Kenna would burst into tears or go for his sister with her tiny manicured nails. He was mildly disappointed she did neither.

Instead Kenna turned her chair, so that she was facing Hannah and raised her chin. "Name them."

"Who?"

"The people you are accusing me of plagiarizing. Name them, please."

"I don't know their names off hand but—"

"I thought not. Who the hell do you think you are? My content is my own—the work I have put into curating an online presence for *Homefires* has been a work of passion. Why on earth would I copy someone else? Did you consider that we have been so successful that those influencers might have been copying *us*?"

Hannah stared back at her with open dislike. "Well that's easily checkable by the dates posted."

"Except you can't name one of them, can you? So, your baseless accusations are just that. Baseless. Perhaps you're just jealous of the fact I get to spend time with Finn and Aiden, and you're stuck in that ivory tower in New York—"

"—Kenna, that's *enough.*" Finn was shocked at the malice in her voice. "Han, can you give us a minute?"

Hannah, far from being upset, looked almost amused. "Sure thing, bro. But not too long or I might get jealous."

Finn hid a laugh in a cough, but he shut the door behind his sister. Kenna had turned back to her computer and was typing furiously, stamping her fingers onto the keyboard.

"Kenna. Kenna, look at me."

He saw her sigh, clench her hands into fists and turn to him. "Kenna… what the hell is going on with you? Do you think it's appropriate to be talking to my sister like that?"

"She just—"

"—I haven't finished." God, he hated confrontation, but this was ridiculous. "There's been other things."

"I know what you think of me. Ever since Lisa; ever since the homeless man." Kenna's voice quivered but Finn wasn't moved.

"You lash out," he said simply. "When you're cornered, you lash out. Do you think Aiden and I don't talk? He told me that you thought I hate you."

"It seems as if you do. You're constantly criticizing me."

Finn pulled up a chair and sat down to face her. It suddenly occurred to him it might look as if he was bullying her, standing over her. "I disagree with you."

"That's how it feels." She sniffed, dashed a stray tear away, but still, Finn felt as if she were putting on a performance for him. *Be fair, give her a chance.*

He hesitated to ask the question he really wanted to ask. "Kenna… the other day at my apartment… in the bathroom. What was that?"

"What was what?"

He waited and to her credit, Kenna didn't smirk. Instead, two spots of pink formed high on her cheeks and tears pooled in her brown eyes.

"Kenna…"

"Don't you know?"

She said it so quietly that he barely heard her. "Know what?" It was getting hard to keep a lid on his frustration.

Kenna looked up at him from under her lashes. "You must know. I know it's inappropriate but… I see you here, every day, being such an inspiration to everyone, being a genius cook and I…"

Finn got up in alarm. *No way. No freaking way.* "Kenna, I think we'd better stop this conversation before it goes any further. Better just say… I expect you to be more civil in your interactions with my staff, my family and our customers." God, he sounded like an old man, a stuffy, corporate old man instead of the young, forward-thinking boss he so wanted to be.

But, Jesus, she was manipulative. "Do you understand?"

She nodded. "I do, and I apologize. I'll apologize to Hannah. You and Aiden have been very kind letting me stay with you."

"Fine." With a breath of relief, Finn opened the door, just to stop the feeling of being smothered that came over him. It was a horrible familiar feeling that made the scars on his chest feel tight. "I'll see you later."

# Chapter Fifteen

Frustrated, Aiden rolled off Finn and sighed. "Really?"

"Sorry, babe. I'm just not feeling it,"

"Clearly." Aiden got out of bed and went to the bathroom, the slight slam of the door telling Finn that his lover was pissed. He couldn't blame him. It had been days since they'd had sex and Finn knew exactly the reason.

Kenna.

In his mind, he'd built her up as an insidious monster, like a quivering spider waiting in the corner of a room, watching, waiting to capture her prey. He'd made the mistake of saying that to Aiden a few nights previously, making him angry.

"For the love of fuck, Finn, why do you do this? *Every* fucking time."

"What do you mean every fucking time?"

Aiden had calmed himself. They had been in the bedroom, Kenna asleep on the couch and Hannah in the guest room.

"What I mean, Finn, is that when everything is going great, you look for anything to prove that you're not meant to be happy. Anything."

Finn was stung. "That's not true."

"I think if you were being honest, you know it's true. You never think you're deserving of happiness. And I get it, I do, after what happened to you. But you're victimizing a young kid this time and I won't have it. Do you know the trouble we could get in if she makes a complaint?"

"I haven't done anything—" But Finn couldn't finish his sentence. He knew Aiden was right and although he, Finn, hadn't done anything to bully or harass Kenna, he could absolutely see how she could twist it. He didn't want to give her anything to use against him.

At work, the tension between Finn and Aiden was beginning to tell on the atmosphere in the kitchen. Even Berto and Clyde were quiet. Worse was to come when Miko, their pastry chef, gave Finn her notice.

"I'm sorry, Finn, but the commute from Oakland is killing me and I can't afford to rent somewhere closer."

"We could help."

Miko had hugged him. "You're sweet but you can't afford to pay what I'd need to live closer and I wouldn't ask you to. I'm sorry, buddy."

So, Finn was distracted by trying to find a new pastry chef, but before he could begin, Hannah's visit was coming to an end. He went with her to the airport and they sat in one of the cafes while they waited for her flight.

Hannah studied her brother. "What's up?"

"Aiden thinks I'm being paranoid. About Kenna, I mean." Finn shook his head. "What do you think?"

Since their argument, Hannah and Kenna had avoided each other and were quietly civil when they did meet. But now Hannah grimaced and fixed her brother with a steady gaze. "She's a snake and I don't think it's paranoid to be wary of her. She blatantly *did* copy that other artist's work and then claim it as her own. She strikes me as someone who will lie and lie until even *she* doesn't know the truth. Watch your back."

As they walked to the gate, Hannah stopped him. "If you want to take it further... talk to her old roommate."

Finn rocked back a little. "I'll keep that in my back pocket, I think. At this point, Aiden will go off if I went that far. It would be an invasion of privacy." He shook his head. "God, Han, maybe I *am* taking her too seriously."

"Hmm." Hannah grimaced and then laughed. "Maybe I shouldn't be encouraging you. I just..." She chuckled and looked away and Finn was shocked to see there were tears in her eyes.

"What is it?"

Hannah collected herself. "You trusted me with something serious. I'm not used to that, not with you." She looked down at her hands. "None of us were. I know Mom and Dad didn't exactly deserve your trust, and it wasn't something I ever thought you would give me. But you did."

"Of course I did." Finn said, with feeling. "You were the only person before Aiden who ever told me that I should be who I wanted to be; who I truly was. God, Hannah, I wouldn't have gotten through what Jack did to me without you."

Hannah pulled him into a bear hug then, and Finn tightened his arms around her.

"You'll come back soon?"

"I will. And you and Aiden come stay with me in New York. Promise?"

"I promise."

He released her then and Hannah grinned. "Eww, we got mushy."

"Live with it."

She nodded, but then her smile faded a little. "Don't let that little snake ruin what you have. You've built a life here, Finn, and a career. That's really something. I'm so proud of my little brother."

Finn was still thinking about that when he took a cab back home. Hannah was right. He and Aiden were good; they were strong. Kenna was nothing more than an irritant and soon, with luck, they wouldn't even need her at the restaurant.

But for now, Aiden was all that mattered. When he got back to the apartment, he sought his lover out. Aiden was sitting out on the small balcony, a half-empty mug of coffee beside him. Finn ran his hands down both of Aiden's thickly-muscled arms. "Hey."

Aiden looked up at him, surprise in his eyes. "Hey. Hannah get off okay?"

"Yup." Finn leaned his cheek against Aiden's head. "Let's go out, babe. Spend the day doing touristy stuff, eating our body weight in junk food and making out like teenagers."

Finn felt Aiden's chuckle rumble through his big body. "You think?"

"I do. Then I'll get you good and relaxed, show you a good time."

Aiden's hands, which had moved to cover Finn's, tightened a little. "Well, you'd better." He kept his tone light, but Finn could tell he was relieved. Aiden stood up. "Where d'you want to go?"

In the end, they took the Alcatraz and Angel Island boat out from Pier 33, mixing in with tourists from all over the world and chatting with the National Parks tour guide. As they walked around the prison and then outside in the restored historical gardens, Aiden and Finn bickered about which of them was Nicolas Cage and who was Sean Connery.

"Obviously, *I'm* Sean," Aiden insisted. "Older guy—"

"Ancient."

"*Older.*" Aiden glared at a grinning Finn. "More worldly wise. You're the idealist."

Even Finn couldn't argue with that.

The views from the Rock were staggering. Finn shook his head as they looked out over the Bay. It was warm, even with the sea breeze, and the sun shone down, turning the red paint of the Golden Gate into liquid metal.

"How come we waited so long to do this?"

"We've been busy, K.B." Aiden grinned at him. "But we could kick back now, take some time to chill. I've been thinking… maybe now we're really getting a foothold in the district, we could hire in some more chefs, mentor them. Take a step back." He chuckled. "Hell, maybe even open a second location."

"You serious?"

Aiden's eyes were soft. "Why not? We can do anything we set our minds to, right?"

"Right… who was the idealist again?"

"Shut up." But Aiden was smiling.

The sun was setting on the ride back to the city and they strolled along Fisherman's Wharf. Finn imagined one of the restaurants having a *Homefires* sign outside and when they went into one of the diners to eat, they sat at the open windows and looked out, people watching.

Yeah, he could imagine opening up here. They both ordered Dungeness Crab with truffle and parmesan fries, Finn requesting a cocktail with his, Aiden sticking to iced tea. Finn sipped his Mojito a little guiltily. "You ever miss it? Booze?"

Aiden shrugged. "Sometimes, sure. Sometimes, when we're sitting out on our balcony, I think it would be nice to have a glass of *Johnny Walker Blue* and a Cuban cigar."

Finn smiled. "It's a nice thought, but you worked so hard to get to this point. It wouldn't be worth the few minutes of pleasure."

"I suppose."

A tiny, almost imperceptible ribbon of worry started in Finn's chest, but he tamped it down. "You *know* it." He kept his tone light, but when they ordered a second round of drinks, he asked for an iced tea too.

After they'd eaten, Aiden started for the parking lot where he'd left the Harley, but Finn shook his head. "Come hold my hand and let's go for a walk. Moonlight stroll."

Aiden snorted but gamely took his hand. "What's with the mushy romance?"

"What, I can't enjoy alone time with my boyfriend?"

Aiden rolled his eyes and didn't push it. Finn was relieved. He didn't want Aiden to know that going home, seeing Kenna there...

god, he just didn't want to see her. If he could just keep Aiden out late enough…

The apartment was quiet and dark when they returned. Aiden moved toward the kitchen, but Finn stopped him, grinning, and drew him into the bedroom. Aiden chuckled as Finn started to undress him. "You need to drink more, Fin-bob Drunk-pants."

"Ssh, I'm giving you my best moves. And I'm not drunk, just horny."

They kissed hungrily, Aiden's hands at the fly of Finn's jeans. When they were naked—not without a lot of laughing as they fumbled and tripped over each other as they made their way to the bed—Finn wrestled a grinning Aiden to the mattress, burying his face in his neck, kissing his throat. Aiden ran his hands up and down Finn's back, cupping his buttocks.

"Ever tell you you're damn sexy, Finn Mason?"

Finn never got to answer as the bedroom was suddenly flooded in light and a banshee cry was given that made them both leap off the bed in alarm.

"What the actual fuck?"

It took a moment to realize that Kenna was in their room, a rolling pin held high above her head, her tiny body contorted in what she must have imagined was a threatening stance. The three of them stared at each other for a long confused moment. Then Kenna lowered her weapon. "Oh. I'm sorry. I thought… I thought someone was robbing us."

Finn gaped at her while Aiden, with more presence of mind, grabbed the comforter to shield his still-erect penis from view. Finn cupped himself quickly.

"No… just us."

Was that a smirk on Kenna's face? If it was, it disappeared just as quickly.

"I'm sorry. I just got scared… you didn't say hi when you came in. Sorry. I'll, um…" She backed out and shut the door.

Aiden looked at Finn and for a moment, Finn just shook his head. Then he laughed, Aiden following suit and then it was all they could do, busting up until tears rolled down their faces. Finn flopped back down on the bed, Aiden beside him.

"Did you see the rolling pin?"

"She could take someone out… by hitting him on the ankle."

Finn snorted. "Guess we don't need a guard dog."

Aiden grinned over at him. "Still feeling horny?"

"Less, I have to admit." Finn pulled a face but Aiden, still smiling, rolled over and kissed him.

"Let me see what I can do about that, gorgeous."

The ridiculousness of the situation the night before made Finn relax more. Kenna was nothing more than a minor irritant, and seeing her brandishing their old, battered rolling pin was such a comical sight, he couldn't take her seriously any more.

He was distracted by having to find a new pastry chef during the following days and when finally, he'd narrowed his picks down to three, he called them all in for a kitchen test during an evening service.

The first guy failed to turn up but when the second one, Greg, arrived Finn smiled at him. "Kiddo, your chances just doubled. Show me what you got."

Greg, a rangy blonde in his early twenties, worked quickly and quietly and his desserts rivalled Miko's so much that by the end of the evening, Finn knew he'd found his man.

"Stay behind after," he told Greg. "We have a staff meal together and you can really get to know everyone."

Finn prepared the usual Friday night vat of his special mac-and-cheese (his staff's favorite), complete with three different strong cheeses and freshly-shaved truffle. He baked fresh, crusty bread and when the restaurant was closed and the kitchen cleaned, they all sat down to eat.

"Hey, is Kenna still here?" Aiden looked up as Finn spoke, and shrugged.

"No idea. I'll go see."

Finn nodded at the dish of mac-and-cheese. "Dig in, pals." He smiled at Greg, who looked shy, a pink flush high on his cheeks. "You good?"

"Yeah, thanks. Is this something you do every night?"

"Most, although usually we make something quicker than this. Fridays, we kick back. The weekend is our busiest time, so it's a nice way to start. Did you enjoy the service?"

Greg nodded. "The places I've worked before, it's been a tense atmosphere." He grinned. "The bosses I've worked for have been way less friendly, which I get. You need to lead, but there are the head chefs who don't want to teach, they want to have power. In my opinion, it affects the quality of the food. It's not like that here."

"Man." Finn was moved. "Thanks. So, could you see yourself working here? Nah, scratch that: I'd like you to think about it before you answer. Just enjoy the meal and let me know over the weekend."

Aiden returned then, with Kenna in tow. Finn nodded over to them. "Greg, this is Kenna, our social media coordinator. Kenna, Greg, whom I hope will be our newest team member."

Kenna nodded at Greg with a disinterested smile and sat down. Finn noticed Greg's face register surprise, then recognition, before he quickly looked away. Finn frowned.

"You know each other?" He asked in a quiet voice, but Greg shook his head and changed the subject. Finn didn't press the matter and later, when he shook Greg's hand, the other man thanked him and left without another word.

At home in bed, Finn was distracted again, and Aiden looked over at him. "'S'up?"

"Ah, nothing. I was hoping Greg would take the job straight away. He fit in real good, don't you think?"

"Yes, he's a good kid, and his zabaglione was sensational. Man, I could eat that twice over."

Finn snorted. "Type II Diabetes, here you come."

"Hey, let me have one vice, at least." Aiden said it mildly, and Finn laughed.

"Fair enough. But I kinda hoped he would say 'Hell yeah, I'll take the job, I'll even start tomorrow'."

"Wishful thinking."

"I thought he might."

They lay in silence for a while. It had started to rain hard outside, and they listened to it hitting the windows with an increasing ferocity.

"Well, at least we won't be attacked by Kenna wielding a rolling pin tonight."

"I replaced it with a baguette," Aiden said, making Finn laugh, "although I can think of something else you could use as a weapon." He grinned lasciviously and nodded down at his very obvious erection. Finn grinned.

"Man, you *really* have to work on your seduction technique."

Aiden grunted and rolled on top of Finn, who smoothed his hands down Aiden's back. "We've been together way too long for that now."

"Ah, romance." But Finn nevertheless kissed him back, their mouths hungry for each other. No interruptions tonight—instead, they made love until both were sated and relaxed.

After Aiden smoothed the damp hair from Finn's forehead, he smiled down at him.

"You know I love the bones of you, right, Finn Mason?"

Finn nodded. "I do. And I love you too."

Aiden smiled and kissed him softly. "We could take the next step, you know."

"Get a dog?"

Aiden laughed and Finn grinned. "No, doofus. We could get married."

Finn stopped, staring up at his lover. "You're serious?"

"Why not? I never thought I cared enough to get married, but with you… I want us to be forever, you know that, right?"

"And we are." Finn put his hands on Aiden's face, "We don't need some official piece of paper to tell us that. You and me. End game."

Aiden half-smiled. "But you don't want to be legally tied to me?"

"We are legally tied, through the restaurant, remember?"

Aiden rolled off of him, but it wasn't in anger. He propped himself up on his elbow, smiling down at him. "In name, I suppose, yes."

"More than in name. It's our legacy, the culmination of both of our hard work."

Aiden nodded. "But then what?"

"What do you mean?"

"Yeah, the restaurant is a success… so now what? We've reached the pinnacle of what we are? Of what our relationship is?"

Finn frowned. "You think marriage is the next step?"

Aiden sighed and rubbed his face. "I don't know. It just seemed… aww, hell, Finn, I don't know. Maybe I'm just… overthinking things." He stared at his lover for a second. "Does it scare you?"

"Marriage?" Finn shrugged. "It's just something I never aspired to. Don't get me wrong, I like that we have the choice now. Doesn't mean it's for me. We've never discussed it before—why now?"

"I don't know. I guess I'm just making sure you're open to it, that… your past hasn't made it so you're scared of committing to one person. To me."

Finn looked away, up at the blank ceiling and said nothing for a few minutes. "I can't answer that right now, Aiden. I just need you to trust that I love you and I'm in this."

For a moment, he wondered if Aiden would go off, would get annoyed. Instead, Aiden laid his hand gently on Finn's chest.

"I can live with that," he said softly. "Yes, Finn Mason, I can live with that."

# Chapter Sixteen

*Whitewater, Kentucky*

*Fourteen years ago…*

The motel manager knew their faces by now, and every time they checked in for the night, he would give them a disgusted yet leering grin. "Enjoy yourselves, boys."

"Ignore him," Jack said as they walked to the room, a new one for them, along the front of the motel. The room was dark, and the overhead light didn't work. Jack went to the nightstand and switched on the lamp. Finn watched him.

"You've been in this room before?"

"Once or twice."

Finn felt a jolt of jealousy shoot through him. His eyes slid to the bed. How many other men—boys—had Jack fucked here? Jack was watching him, an amused smile on his handsome face. "Finn… you're the first lover I've brought here, don't worry." He sighed, unbuckling his belt. "I used to come here to get away from my wife whenever she had one of her girl's evenings. Shrieking harpies." He shuddered, unaware that Finn was staring at him with horror.

"You were *married*?"

Jack looked up, finally registering Finn's shock. He sighed and shifted towards him, sliding his arms around his waist. "Still am. Technically. She went back west a couple of years ago, saying she couldn't pretend any more. Can't say I blame her."

He leaned forward to give a kiss, but Finn stepped back out of his arms.

"What is it?"

Finn felt sick. "You're married."

"Yes. It has nothing to do with us, Finn, my love. Nothing."

Finn suddenly felt very young. Jack was a married man, twice his age. What the hell were they doing here?

"Hey, hey, hey, it's okay." Jack came to him again and this time Finn didn't back away. "You are my world, Finn. When I met you, something shifted inside me. I had to hold back, because I was your teacher, I was in a position of responsibility. But now we are both free to love. You and I, Finn, we are forever."

He kissed Finn, and then they were in bed and Finn was on his stomach, giving himself over to the pleasure of Jack's tongue inside him. As his cock slid into him, Finn closed his eyes and let go.

As they made love, Jack's mouth on his neck, his teeth biting into his shoulder, Finn let his doubts go. As his orgasm exploded through him, he heard Jack's voice, his whisper.

"Promise me we're forever, Finn Mason, promise me you'll never leave me. I would die if you left me."

"I promise..."

"Say it again.... Say it again my love... I'll never let you go..."

# Chapter Seventeen

*San Francisco*
*Present day…*

To Finn's great relief, Aiden didn't press the subject of marriage, nor did he seem to be harboring any ill-will toward his partner for his rejection of the idea.

The week passed in a rush of work and it wasn't until the following Sunday morning that Finn called Greg to see if he would take the job. He was pretty confident the young man would agree, so confident in fact that when Greg gently turned him down, it was a palpable shock.

"I'm sorry, Finn, I just don't think I'd be the right fit."

Finn took a deep breath. "I have to say I disagree, and I thought… What changed your mind?"

Greg gave him a bland excuse and Finn sensed he wasn't hearing the whole story. "Of course, I respect your decision, but I have to say I'm disappointed. Your skills really would have elevated our menu."

"I'm sorry, Finn." To his credit, Greg really did sound regretful. Finn took a shot.

"Look, meet me for lunch today. Give me another shot at persuading you. Please."

There was a long silence on the end of the line then: "Okay. But not at *Homefires.*"

Finn breathed out in relief. "No problem." He named a place in the city and arranged a time.

He half-expected Greg to stand him up, but when Finn arrived at the restaurant, he was already waiting, a tall glass of lemonade in front of him. The young man looked nervous as Finn greeted him. Finn grinned: "I promise, I'm not going to coerce you into anything. I just want to know why, when we seemed to really hit it off on Friday. I know the whole team thought so too. So, what gives?"

Greg looked down at his hands for a long moment, then back at Finn. "I had no idea that Kenna Mitchell worked for you."

Finn's heart sank. "You know her?"

"I know *of* her." Greg stressed. He stopped then shook his head. "Finn, I wanted the job. So badly you wouldn't believe it, but knowing she's there…"

"Tell me why."

Greg flushed red. "It's not my place."

"Yes, it is. Greg… I shouldn't be saying this, but I have my own issues with Kenna. If she's a threat to my business, I need to know."

"Look, it isn't even my story to tell." Greg looked uncomfortable but there was no way Finn would let him leave without telling him something. By Greg's expression, he sensed that he *wanted* to tell him.

"Between us?"

"Scout's honor." Finn signaled the waiter. "Let's grab some food and talk."

They ordered a platter of popcorn shrimp and a jug of iced tea. "Tell me everything."

Greg sighed. "You know a club called *Deviance* in the city?"

Finn shook his head. "Doesn't ring a bell. Does that make me old?"

"No, it makes you guilty of good taste." Greg shuddered. "My roommate worked the bar there. It's ostensibly a straight club, but over the years it's become more inclusive of everyone, the bi-curious, especially. It started to have gay-only nights a couple of years ago, but even then, straight clients would still go. Kenna Mitchell was, and as far as I know, still is, a client."

"Client? Not customer?"

Greg smirked without humor. "Maybe I should say predator. Kenna's known for going after who she wants. Straight, gay, it doesn't matter."

"That, in itself, isn't a rare thing. What makes Kenna so different?" Finn was trying to be fair, but his heart was thudding hard against his ribs. He wanted to know more and yet didn't at the same time.

"What she does when she doesn't get what she wants! I don't think Kenna has ever paid her own way, at least, not according to my friend. She couch surfs for a while, then somehow, makes her way into the bed of whoever her mark is. And she's not shy about it."

Greg took out his cellphone and flicked to an Instagram page. Finn looked at the name at the top and didn't recognize it, but as he scrolled down and saw the photos, he let out a sigh.

Kenna wasn't shy about exposing her body, that was for sure. In some of the photos she wore little more than a leather harness, her body posed awkwardly in what Finn assumed she thought was a seductive position.

Then she was wrapped around a beautiful boy as they both pouted for a selfie; another image showed her draped over a chair, her perfectly rounded buttocks towards the camera and nothing hidden. Kenna looked back over her shoulder, her wide brown eyes heavily made up, her mouth open coquettishly. It was a sensual yet unnerving photograph—there was something of the Lolita in how she posed and what she was clearly offering. Finn felt a little sick.

"So, she's a narcissist."

"Yup. Now, bear in mind, what I'm about to tell you is second-hand from my roommate." Greg sighed and took a moment to eat some shrimp. Finn sipped his iced tea.

"My roommate's cousin, Brooks, came to stay with us a year ago. He was a great kid, shy but a great sense of humor and we loved having him there. He settled in Frisco, eventually he rented his own place with a guy he'd met. My roommate had gotten him a job tending bar at the club and he kinda liked the whole vibe there, the inclusivity, the open-mindedness." Greg gave a little chuckle and shook his head. "Brooks was an innocent, Finn. He didn't see the passive-aggression, the manipulation. He and Kenna became friends and eventually, she moved in with them, saying her own roommate was a psycho who she couldn't get away from. We never found out if that was true."

He rubbed his face. "Now, I have to say this. We don't know exactly what happened, but it all started to go wrong for Brooks when she moved in. We tried to reach him but he became incredibly insular and withdrawn."

Finn didn't want to ask, but it was inevitable. "What happened?"

Greg took a slug of tea, coughed as it went the wrong way. "He jumped off the Golden Gate bridge a few months ago."

"Jesus."

Greg nodded. "Kenna didn't even bother to attend the funeral. In fact, I was told, she was back at the club, looking for her next victim. Brooks didn't leave a note or any indication why he jumped, but his boyfriend told us he found Kenna and Brooks in bed together the night before. Kenna didn't even apologize; in fact, she found it funny. She found it *funny*." Greg cussed under his breath and stared out of the window.

Finn felt the familiar tightness come back into his chest; he was revolted, disgusted and yet he needed to know more. Before he could ask though, Greg looked at him.

"You know that story of the kid whose girlfriend talked him into killing himself?"

Finn nodded. "Back in New England, right?"

"Right." Greg drew in a shaky breath. "Brooks' boyfriend told us that after he found them in bed together, Brooks begged his forgiveness, but he made him sleep on the couch. He heard an argument between Brooks and Kenna, which petered out in the early hours, but he heard them whispering. He thinks she was trying to talk him into jumping. All he heard was, 'It only takes four seconds and no more pain'. In context, what else could she have meant? The next night, Brooks jumped, and Kenna moved her stuff out, not even saying thanks or goodbye, or even expressing any sympathy. Like she'd done with them; they were no longer of use."

"Does she still go to the club?"

"That, I don't know. I never went back, and my roommate quit the day of Brooks' funeral. When I saw her at your place, I felt sick. God, I felt like throwing up, but I couldn't say anything. She doesn't know me, at least, she didn't seem to recognize me, and I couldn't risk her doing so." He looked at Finn. "Man, get her out – of your restaurant, your life. I don't know if she's part of your social circle but—"

"—she's currently in our guest room."

Greg shook his head. "Hell, Finn... *no.* She looks innocent but she's insidious. A real narcissist." He looked regretful. "Man, I hate to leave it like that because I have no proof. She's clever, a master manipulator. She will make you believe you're the one in the wrong, that she's just this... fuck. I try not to hate, Finn, but she's the exception. I can't take the job. I'm sorry but I won't expose me or my loved ones to that poison."

Finn felt as if he had been slammed by a wrecking ball. "I hate to lose you. If... and I know it's a big if, if you're still available when Kenna... leaves..."

Greg smiled. "Then call me. I'd give anything to work with you – except deal with Kenna."

Finn left the restaurant and for a while he just walked, not really seeing where he was going. So many emotions were flooding his system that he felt disconnected from the world somehow. Greg had confirmed, pretty much, his suspicions about Kenna, though Finn knew he was only hearing one side of the story.

But he knew in his bones that Greg was being honest. *Jesus…* Suddenly Finn didn't want to go home. This was too much, too close to what he had gone through before. Every feeling of not being in control, of being played and trapped came back to him, and as he walked through the streets. He didn't even feel the hot sun pounding down on him, or the noise of the street vendors. He just felt… numb.

"Hey, man."

Finn looked up to see a handsome African-American man smiling at him. He looked vaguely familiar. Finn blinked. "Hey."

The man chuckled. "Guess you don't remember me? Olly. Olly Roberts. When you saw me last, I was wearing a uniform."

*Ah, right, the fire chief.* Finn shook himself back into the present. "Oh, yeah, of course; I'm sorry."

"You okay, man? You looked out of it?"

Finn half-smiled. "Just got a lot on my mind. How are you?"

"Good, yeah." He asked how the restaurant was doing, and as they chatted, Finn noticed for the first time how attractive the other man was. *Huh.* He noticed other guys, of course, but his heart had been so wrapped up in Aiden for the last few years, that it was never more than a cursory glance.

But Olly Roberts was a damn fine looking man. His chocolatey-warm eyes twinkled with good humor and kindness, and the sculpted planes of his face were softened by a neatly-clipped beard and the warm caramel of his skin. He smiled at Finn now. "Hey, you want to go grab a drink?"

Finn really did want to grab a drink with this guy, but he shook his head. "I'm sorry. I'd like to but…"

"Gotcha. No problem. See you around." Olly clapped him on the back and took off, grinning a goodbye. Finn wanted to go after him, change his mind. Olly was a complication and yet he was uncomplicated and that was so appealing right now.

Eventually, though, he had to go back to the apartment. As he opened the door, he heard laughter coming from the living room. Irritation flooded through him, which got worse when he walked in and saw both Aiden and Kenna stretched out on the floor, laying on their bellies playing a card game. An empty bottle of wine lay on its side on the table.

"Hi."

They both looked up at him, and Aiden smiled, but neither got up. "Hey, cutie. Take a pew—we're playing."

"I can see." Finn gave them a chilly smile, not meeting Kenna's gaze, and walked into the kitchen. Aiden followed him a moment later.

"You okay?"

"Sure."

Aiden frowned. "Could you make that convincing?"

"Sorry. Greg didn't take the job."

"Damn… welp, can't be helped." Aiden grinned at his rhyme, but Finn just rubbed his face.

Aiden slid a hand onto the back of Finn's neck. "Seriously, K.B., what's up?"

Finn sighed, not wanting this conversation with Kenna only a few feet away. He nodded in the direction of her, however. "You've been drinking?"

Aiden's eyes narrowed. "No. The wine is Kenna's."

"Just asking."

Aiden turned and closed the door, before turning back to his lover. "The fuck is up with you? And don't give me that crap about Greg. What's going on?" His eyes flicked to the door, then his expression changed. "You jealous?"

Finn laughed. "Of *her*? Why, should I be?"

"Don't be fucking ridiculous. We were just killing time. If you gave her a chance—" Finn snorted and Aiden sighed. "Yeah, well, let me know when you're done being a paranoid baby."

Aiden left the kitchen, only slamming the door a little and Finn shook his head. Come on now, be a man. Stand your ground. Just go out there and tell Kenna she needs to find somewhere else to live.

As he opened the door however, he heard the front door to the apartment close. He frowned. "Aiden?"

No answer. He checked the living room—empty. Aiden had left. With Kenna? Finn went to the window and looked down the street. Sure enough, he saw his lover striding away from the apartment building, Kenna practically running to match his big stride. As they turned a corner, Finn saw Kenna look back and although it was some distance, he could have sworn she was smirking.

"You little *bitch*." He hissed the words out, and it made him feel better, if for only a moment. *Fuck this shit.* He thought of the boy who had jumped from the Golden Gate, and John, whose only crime was to be homeless. He thought of Lisa. They had to be connected, there wasn't any doubt in his mind.

So, fuck Kenna Mitchell. He was going to expose her if it cost him everything.

# Chapter Eighteen

Finn used the time he had alone in the apartment to check out any news he could find on the Internet about recent suicides from the Golden Gate. There were plenty about Lisa, of course, and his heart pounded with sadness as he looked at the photographs of his lost friend. "I'm so sorry, Lisa."

The thought that Kenna may have had something to do with Lisa's suicide made him furious. He scrolled through the search results and found three articles on local news sites. The first merely mentioned Brook's name, the fact he was from a small town near Bakersfield, California, and that he had come to San Francisco to find work. No mention of a note, his sexuality or even his family.

The second article gave a little more. There was a funeral date and place given, and the fact he was survived by his boyfriend and his family. There was a photograph showing a distraught young man being supported by another. Finn recognized Greg and his heart went out to him. God. Such loss. He remembered how he had felt at Lisa's funeral—confusion at the futility of it all.

The third article even had a quote from Brooks' boyfriend. *He was driven to it…* Those words kept coming back to Finn now as he closed his laptop, sickened. What the hell was he going to do? Without proof, Aiden would not listen to him. Meanwhile, Kenna would continue to inveigle herself into their lives.

He looked at the clock. The restaurant wasn't open tonight, but he really didn't want to be in the apartment when Aiden and Kenna got back, smirking at him. *Screw the both of them.*

He grabbed his jacket and his phone and headed out of the door. He took the bus to the restaurant, and went inside, locking the door behind him. Upstairs in the office, he pulled out the personnel files and check out the address Kenna had given them at the start. He tapped it into a note on his phone and looked through the rest of the file. No more detail than necessary legally, he noticed. She gave her name, address, social security number, bank details.

She hadn't even needed to fill in an application form. What had he been thinking? Had she done this in every job? What kind of casualty list had Kenna left behind in her wake? And what the hell kind of person was she, really?

Finn called a cab to take him to her previous address. When he got there, he leaned on the buzzer until an irate female voice crackled through the intercom. "The fuck? What do you want?"

"I'm here about Kenna Mitchell."

The disembodied voice laughed without mirth. "She doesn't live here any more, thank *fuck.*"

"Wait… I'm here about her. I need to know some things."

There was a long silence and Finn wasn't sure if she had hung up. Then the door buzzed. "Come up."

The apartment building had no elevator and so Finn climbed the five flights to the apartment. He saw the roommate—or ex-roommate—leaning on the open door jamb. She was tall, pretty, her dark hair tied up in a ponytail, her black t-shirt revealing elaborate tattoo sleeves on each arm. Her expression was less than friendly. "You friends with her?"

It was Finn's turn to give a sarcastic laugh. "Hell, no."

The roommate thawed a little, and she stood aside to let him in. The apartment was airy and clean. A vape pen sat on a side table next to an empty coffee mug. "You want a drink?"

"Thanks."

"Coffee?"

"White, no sugar, thanks."

She nodded to the couch. "Have a pew. I'm Hayley, by the way."

"Finn. Finn Mason."

She smiled now. "Cool. I'll be right back, Finn-Finn."

Finn relaxed. A couple of minutes later, she was back and handing him a steaming cup. "So, what can I tell you about Kenna? Depends on what you want to know. And why. So… why?"

Finn sipped his coffee before answering. He met Hayley's gaze evenly. "I think she's trash. She works for me—at the moment—and ever since she's been there, things have been happening. Bad things."

"How bad are we talking? Stealing or actual bodily harm?" Hayley clearly didn't beat around the bush and Finn appreciated that.

"Both. Well, the stealing thing is hard to prove, but we think—I think—that she's been stealing other influencers' artwork and ideas."

"You're right, that is hard to prove but right on brand for Kenna."

"That's what I thought." He sighed and put his cup down. "What's worse is… and I'm aware I may sound like Paranoid

Android here, but I think she's linked to a couple of deaths. One of my chefs jumped to her death, and a homeless man died in a fire outside my restaurant. Both since Kenna started with us." He gave a half-chuckle. "Yeah, I know what it sounds like."

"It sounds about par for the course."

Hayley's words were simple, but the confirmation of his fears provoked a sudden and somewhat embarrassing reaction in Finn.

He burst into tears. Once he started, he could not stop, and it was only after a moment that he realized Hayley had moved and put her arm around his shoulders. When he had calmed himself, she spoke. "Don't feel bad. This is what she does. She's insidious. I bet she had some tales about me."

"She said you were a psycho who stole her stuff."

Hayley hooted with laughter, which made Finn feel better. He quickly wiped his eyes. "Sorry about that."

"Don't be. Like I said, this is what she drives a person to. Luckily for me, I've always been an ornery bitch, so in the end she gave up gaslighting me. She made some trouble for me at my job – well, she tried, but luckily my boss is even more of a hard ass than I am."

"What's your job?"

Hayley grinned and held out her arms. "Take a look." The tattoos were extraordinary and now, as he studied them, he saw a very familiar quotation. He sighed and took out his phone.

"Take a look."

Hayley looked at the restaurant's Instagram feed and saw what Finn was talking about. A photograph of a framed text that Kenna had put up in her office. "Ha. *Per aspera ad astra*. Through adversity to the stars." She looked at him kindly. "I can't accuse her of stealing that, it wasn't mine to begin with but, yeah, the font she used, the format. Girl can't come up with an original idea if she tried."

She patted his shoulder. "You driving?"

He shook his head. "You got somewhere to be?"

"Nope." He really didn't, he decided, and this girl was nice.

"Then let's drink and bitch about Kenna and figure out a plan of action."

He got home way after midnight. He didn't bother going into the guest room; he didn't trust himself not to drag Kenna and throw her out on her ass. Hayley had told him some of the crap Kenna had done when they lived together and his anger was a boiling, roiling thing inside of him ready to blow.

But he wasn't dumb enough to explode. That's what she wanted. Instead, he would play the long game and get enough evidence to finally convince Aiden to rid their lives of her.

Aiden was asleep or pretending to be asleep. Finn contemplated sleeping on the couch, but he didn't want Kenna to see any rift in their relationship. He undressed and slid into bed, but stayed away from Aiden's body. He was relieved when Aiden didn't touch him. He wanted to keep this anger inside him and harness it. Aiden's touch right now would break him.

*No. Not break.* No-one would or could ever do that to him again. Not after Jack. He, Finn, was a survivor, a warrior.

If Kenna thought she could even compare to what Jack had done in the past, she was very, very wrong.

# Chapter Nineteen

*Whitewater, Kentucky*
*Thirteen years ago…*

Finn waited outside as Jack got the key for the motel room. The weather had been particularly hot over the past weeks and Finn's throat was scratchy from the dust devils that kicked up out on the forecourt of the motel.

He'd started to hate this place. The filthy bedspreads, the smell of stale piss in the bathrooms. The way Jack assumed he was always up for a fuck. He knew he shouldn't blame him; why else did they come here? But lately, Finn felt more and more rebellious. He wanted more than just a weekly fuck. He wanted someone to love openly.

He knew now that person wasn't Jack Boyd. Finn felt guilty, of course. Jack had done so much for him, had helped him accept his own sexuality, giving him the confidence to pursue his dream of being a chef.

Now that dream was going to become a reality. Hannah had moved to New York City six months previously, and now she was in touch with him, telling him to come live with her and take an internship at the restaurant of a head chef she knew.

There was no question in Finn's mind that he would go, but now he had the hardest part to get through. Telling Jack that he was leaving. That he wanted a clean break. Jesus, this was going to be so difficult… and it didn't help that in the car on the way over, he'd smelled liquor on Jack's breath. Again. He also looked wrecked, dark shadows under his watery blue eyes, and he looked… greasy. Finn swallowed hard and tried not to let his distaste show.

As he watched Jack shamble back to him now, he thought how old his lover looked. Jack was barely in his forties and yet…

Jack waved the key. "All good." They walked to their usual room on the corner of the motel.

It stunk even more today or maybe Finn was just looking for things to complain about. Anything to distract himself from what he had to do. He let Jack kiss him, but when he moved towards the bed, he gently pushed him away. "We have to talk."

Jack ran a hand through his thinning hair. "Sure thing. We have all night."

Finn sighed as he watched Jack grab his bag and take out two full bottles of Scotch. No way was he drinking tonight. "Jack… I'm going to New York."

"Oh, yeah? Visiting your sister?"

"*Moving* to New York."

He let that hang in the air while he watched understanding seep into Jack's eyes. "What?"

"I'm moving away from Whitewater. I'm going to New York to live with my sister."

Jack stared at him, and Finn felt the weight of his love again, the suffocating weight of it that had begun to smother him of late.

"You can't."

Finn chewed on his bottom lip. "It's all set, Jack. I'm leaving on Saturday."

"What the fuck? I mean, what the *fuck*, Finn? When were you going to tell me?"

"I'm telling you now. I didn't tell you before because I didn't want to hurt you."

Jack laughed then, but the sound was entirely without humor. "So, what is it you think you're doing here now?"

"I didn't want to be talked out of it. I won't be. I'm sorry, Jack, but we both know this was coming to an end."

Finn was struggling not to let his nerves overcome him—if he did, Jack would sense that weakness and turn on the charm followed by the begging, then finally the passive-aggression that had become so much a part of their relationship lately.

Jack sat down heavily on the bed. Finn sat in one of the chairs and waited. Would Jack explode into one of his rages? Finn was ready for that.

No. Instead Jack just looked at him with endless sorrow in his eyes. "Okay, then. I guess… I guess that's that." He tried to smile. "New York will be good for you. Your sister finding you a job?"

"An apprentice position at a restaurant."

Jack nodded. "Good, that's good. I always said you should go for it, the chef thing. You have a talent that shouldn't be wasted." He gazed at Finn for a long time then stood up and came to him, crouching down in front of him. "I won't pretend that this doesn't hurt."

He slid his hand onto the back of Finn's neck and leaned his forehead against his. "I love you, kiddo. I have since we first met, although obviously, I couldn't tell you then. You and me, these last months… the happiest I've ever been."

He let go of Finn then and stood. "May I ask one last favor?"

"Sure." Finn was feeling the relief of an argument avoided. He'd have agreed to just about anything at that moment.

Jack smiled. "Stay with me one last night. Say goodbye properly."

"Sure, Jack, sure."

He owed it to this man to give him one last night, and so Finn went to bed with Jack and made love with him, entirely focused on giving him as much pleasure as he could.

He wasn't even sure what woke him up first. The acrid smell of smoke or the fact Jack's entire body weight was on top of him and his hands were pushing Finn's face down into the pillow.

He couldn't breathe. Dragging himself from the confusion of sleep, Finn's adrenaline spurred him into action, bucking and arching his body in an effort to get Jack's weight off him. But Jack was way too strong and as Finn struggled, the few times he managed to get his mouth and nose out of the pillow, all he was dragging into his lungs was smoke.

Brief flashes of the room. The drapes were on fire, the easy chair. The cheap television screen looked as if it was curling at the edges in the heat and the bed… the bed was on fire.

"Stop fighting me, my darling. This is how it's supposed to end. You and me… we're meant to be together in life and death…"

He was fucking crazy. Finn gave a roar of terror and managed to push him off enough that he could roll off the bed and onto the floor. He started to crawl, half-blinded by the thick, choking smoke. He heard Jack scream. A searing pain ripped through his chest—he had crawled over a cracked, burning bottle of liquor… it was how Jack had started the fire Finn realized and now there were red hot pieces of glass embedded in his chest … Jack was grabbing at his ankles, pulling him down and back… and the floor…

In his agony, Finn suddenly had the most ridiculous thought… *the floor is lava, the floor is lava.* He and Hannah used to play that game all the time. Except this time, now, the floor really was on fire and he was in it, and his lungs were failing and the adrenaline, the will to fight, to survive was draining from him.

Dark spots crowded in from the edge of his vision and he felt his body shutting down. Dying. He gave one last struggle, but as a sudden rush of light and oxygen flooded into the room and he heard panicked shouting, he gave in to the darkness.

He hadn't expected to wake up. When he felt the pain of his injuries hit, Finn wished he hadn't and when they had to abrade the second-degree burns on his chest, he screamed even though they'd pumped him full of morphine.

Weeks turned into months. It was the first time he'd seen any acts of love from his shocked parents, but soon enough came the recriminations and judgement.

Not from Hannah. She took a sabbatical from work and cared for him when his parents lost interest in looking after him. It was Hannah who told him finally that Jack too had survived, that he had been under police guard since the fire, and that he had been charged with attempted murder.

The press had gotten hold of the story and were camped outside the hospital. His parents sold his story, ostensibly to pay for his medical bills, but it wasn't enough. In the end, out of sheer embarrassment, the school board covered his medical bills in exchange for him keeping quiet.

Finn was more than happy to do that. His life in Whitewater was over and when, after months, he was released from the hospital, he only went back to his parents' house to pack his stuff. Then Hannah took him back to New York to finish his recovery.

Jack's sentencing went ahead the following September. The Whitewater DA had downgraded the charges from attempted murder to attempted manslaughter on account of Finn's refusal to testify and Jack's agreement to plead guilty to the charges. He went to jail, of course, but Finn knew that sooner or later, Jack would be out in the world again.

Jack wrote to him just once, from prison. *Baby, I'm so sorry, I went crazy. Blah, blah, blah.* Every cliched apology he could think of. Finn wasn't impressed, and he certainly didn't respond. Being away from Whitewater helped immeasurably.

Instead, he got better; he recovered. The wounds on his chest healed though the scars, mental and physical, would remain. Eventually, when he was well enough, Hannah hooked him up with her chef friend and Finn hadn't looked back since.

# Chapter Twenty

*San Francisco*
*Present day…*

Finn and Aiden circled each other warily for the next few days, faux politeness the name of the game. Finn ignored Kenna at work and at home, taking himself out of the apartment whenever he could and returning late in the evenings when he could legitimately go straight to bed.

He was getting to know the neighborhood really well on his long walks at night. A few blocks from the apartment, he found an all-night diner where he could hunker down for a few hours with a book and an endless supply of coffee.

It had become a regular thing now and even the waitress behind the counter, Agnes, knew his name. Finn chatted with her a little as she got his latte ready, then he moved to his favorite booth in the corner.

Tonight, it was raining hard outside and there were few people on the streets and in the diner. Finn could hear the radio on in the kitchen, and the endless patter of rain against the windows.

He had brought his laptop along with him tonight and was flicking disinterestedly through a bunch of property listings, hoping to find something Kenna could afford. He wanted her out of the apartment, but he also didn't want to start a fight with Aiden. He was still pissed with his boyfriend, but he hated to fight—and he definitely didn't want to fight in front of Kenna.

He heard the door of the diner open and looked up. He recognized Fire Chief Roberts from the other night—what was his name again? Oliver. *Olly.*

Olly was joking around with the waitress, Aggie, as he ordered food. Finn saw he was still dressed in his work gear, a smudge of dirt or soot high on that sensually gorgeous face.

*Shit.* That was no way to think. Finn was about to look away when Olly looked over and his smile ratcheted up to mind-blowing.

Oh… shit.

Olly thanked Aggie and walked over. "You again."

"Me again." Finn decided to go with it. "Would you like to join me?" *Fuck it, why not?*

"Sure, thanks." Olly slid into the booth, opposite Finn, and grinned at him. "We keep meeting."

"You just get off work?"

"Did the uniform give it away?"

Finn grinned. "And the strategically placed dirt." He pointed to the smudge on Olly's cheek and, chuckling, the other man scrubbed at it with his sleeve.

"Hazards of the job. Don't be too impressed, it was a dumpster fire."

Finn stopped himself from saying, "Just like my life, then." This guy didn't need to know his personal crap. For once, he just wanted to kick back and talk with someone who didn't have anything to do with Kenna Mitchell. "How long have you been a fireman?"

"Fifteen years." Olly grinned at Finn's surprise. "Yeah, I know. I look younger than I am. Truth is, I joined up straight from college; wanted to give back. I got into college on a scholarship, so thought I ought to do something meaningful, you know? What about you?"

"Food is my passion. Was never a choice really. Not that sometimes I wish it was less pressured."

"Well, that's the way it is. You work your ass off for your passion, you'll always find success. Me and the fellas ate at your place a while back."

Finn was surprised. "You did? I didn't see you."

"Think you were hard at it in the kitchen. You and your partner own the place?"

Finn nodded. "Aiden." Why did saying his name hurt, now? Why was there a feeling of dread in his chest? He looked away from Olly's gaze, pretending to be absorbed in his almost empty coffee mug.

"You been together long?"

Finn drew in a long breath. "Yeah. Things… well, you know how it is. You're together a while, things can get…"

Olly grinned. "You ever finish a sentence?"

Finn laughed. "Sure. Just…"

"You don't want to talk about it?"

"Bingo."

Olly nodded. "That's cool. Last time I was in a relationship, if I can remember back that far, nothing bad happened, we just forgot to be excited about each other. In the end, he moved out and I hate to say it, but I barely even noticed. That sounds bad. I did love him at one point."

"You ever see him now?"

"Not so much. Now and again. So, what are you doing out this late? Insomnia?"

Finn looked at him, at that kind, warm, caring face and wanted to tell him everything. Which was ridiculous—the man was a virtual stranger, but soon enough, he was recounting the story of Lisa, John and Kenna. Olly nodded along, his eyes intent on Finn's face.

"John was the homeless guy who died, right?"

"Right. I know the incident report said he died because he was smoking and drinking but he didn't smoke. And just because he was homeless, it didn't mean he'd be careless about his own safety."

"I know. I can't tell you anything, Finn, I'm sorry. But technically, yeah, it could have been… I hate to use the word murder but…"

"Now who isn't finishing their sentences?" But Finn's smile cracked. "Maybe I'm being paranoid, but I just keep hearing worse and worse things about the woman. I don't need that kind of cancer in my life." He stopped, shook his head, gave a half-chuckle. "Sorry, dude. You don't need to hear all of this."

Olly smiled but his eyes were serious. "Listen, man, you have every right to want to protect yourself. If it were just your suspicions, I'd say hang back, but you've heard from more than one source that this girl is trouble. Kick her to the curb."

Finn was buoyed by his words. "Thanks, man."

Olly grinned. "And don't let her hound you out of your own home. Screw her. You don't owe her a place to live." He signaled to

Aggie for a refill of his coffee. "Now, can I talk you into sharing a plate of French fries with me? Even if it's way too late… or way too early, however you look at it."

Finn laughed. "You've got a deal."

It was almost dawn before Finn checked his watched and smiled wryly. "I'd better go home. Don't want Aiden calling the cops on me."

Olly grinned. "Sure. Listen, if you find yourself here, say late Tuesday night, save me a seat."

"I will. Thanks for listening."

Finn smiled at him and said goodbye but before he reached the door, Olly called him back. "I'm serious, Finn. This girl… I've dealt with people like her before. You're right to call her a cancer. Don't let her ruin everything you've built."

At home, Finn closed the front door. No sound, Aiden obviously hadn't waited up for him. *Good.* Finn didn't want to have to explain where he had been all night. He didn't want the pleasant evening ruined, nor have to try to explain who he'd been with. It wasn't like he had been cheating with Olly, just sharing a meal with a friend.

The guest room door was closed, and Finn could see a soft light underneath the door. He went into the living room, closing the door. Shrugging out of his coat, he dumped it on the floor and flopped back onto the couch. Why was it he didn't want to go to bed, didn't want to be around Aiden right now? His skin felt itchy with irritation—he didn't even feel sad. *Fuck this.* In the morning, he would tell Kenna that if she wanted to keep her job, she needed to find somewhere else to live. If Aiden sided with her…

… Finn didn't want to think about that. Instead, he stretched out on the couch, grabbing his jacket and balling it up under his head. Sleep evaded him, however, and the couch was lumpy and uncomfortable. When his elbow hit something hard, Finn reached behind the cushion. A small, gaudily-decorated tin fell into his hands and, curious, he opened it.

The smell hit him first. Dope. A couple of small buds were crammed into the corner of the tin, with cigarette papers and some strands of stale tobacco. Finn's gaze was caught, though, by the three small white pills half hidden under the dope. He recognized them instantly.

*Vicodin.* The drug that had nearly destroyed Aiden's life.

In the morning, he was waiting for Kenna when she came into the kitchen. He'd left the tin on the kitchen counter in plain view. He watched as her eyes took in the box, then flicked to his. With some satisfaction, he saw something like fear flicker in her eyes. Finn kept his voice calm and steady. "You will pack your stuff and be out of this apartment in a half hour. Don't bother coming into the restaurant, we'll send any personal items on to you. You'll be paid a month's salary, and that's it."

Kenna stayed silent but gave a quick nod. Finn's eyes slid to Aiden who had heard the last few words as he came into the kitchen.

"What the hell is going on?"

Finn ignored his lover, instead focusing on the woman in front of him. "Twenty-five minutes, Kenna."

Kenna turned on her heel and stalked out of the kitchen. Aiden looked confused and pissed off. “What the hell, Finn?”

Finn nodded at the tin and Aiden took a look. Finn watched his expression change. “Well, fuck, Finn, it’s just some grass and a couple of pills.”

“In an apartment belonging to an addict.”

“*Ex*-addict, jackass. Jesus, Finn, you really don’t trust me?”

Finn stayed silent, and he saw Aiden almost flinch. “Duly noted.” Then he too turned and left the kitchen. Finn stood still, his chest tight and tense, listening to the low murmur of conversation from Kenna’s room.

Less than ten minutes later, the door to the apartment slammed shut and Finn knew he was alone.

# Chapter Twenty-One

**EatsNGreetsonTheStreets**
**Restaurant Online Review Community**

*HomeFires, Restaurant and Bar, Castro Hill, SF, Reviewed 6th October*
★☆☆☆☆

*Having eaten at the restaurant a few times now, I can honestly say that there is no more disappointing place to eat on the Hill. The gimmick—fine dining in a homely setting—ran out of steam pretty quickly and so now, all the restaurant has to do is maintain the quality of their admittedly impressive-sounding menu.*

*Sadly, as much as I hate to say it, head chef Finn Mason's imagination appears to be as limited as his talent. His cioppino lacks not just seasoning but the fresh taste; San Francisco demands more of one of its favorite dishes and his bouillabaisse is bouilli-basic.*

*Throw in morose and obviously underpaid staff, and the dining experience is less Homefires than it is Dysfunctional-Home. The place's chi is all wrong too. Don't waste your time.*

Did you find this review useful? 👍 Yes 👎 No

👍 514 did find this review useful

👎 658 did not find this review useful

# Chapter Twenty-Two

They'd had bad reviews before, of course, but this one was not only incorrect but spiteful. It didn't take a genius to figure out where it had come from.

Finn saw it and shrugged. "All bullshit, of course." He could tell from the wording that Kenna wanted him to know she was the author. Petty *and* spiteful.

But his crew was demoralized by it, and worse, they had picked up on the tension between him and Aiden. Tension didn't really cover it.

It had been a week since Kenna left and Aiden had barely spoken to Finn. In fairness, Finn wasn't making the effort either, figuring his partner would come around, eventually. He knew Aiden had helped Kenna find somewhere to stay, probably given her money, but right now he was having a hard time caring. As long as Kenna was out of their lives, that was all that mattered. Now they could go on with their lives. Aiden would come around.

Despite the review's summation of the staff's morale, they got over their mood quickly, and the restaurant was busier than ever. Finn knew he had done the right thing firing Kenna when each one of his crew came to tell him quietly that they were relieved.

"I couldn't tell you what bugged me about her," the easy-going Berto said to him quietly, one night a few weeks later, "Just like … you know them big house spiders that you see … they all up in the corner of the room just watching you with those eight creepy-ass eyes of theirs?" He illustrated his point by pulling his arms up and splaying his fingers.

Finn snorted. "You lunatic."

"I mean it. She was always watching us – you mostly." Berto's smile faded. "Lisa really hated her."

Finn's chest tightened. "Did Lisa say anything to you? About Kenna specifically?"

Berto looked uncomfortable. "Ah, man… Lisa made me promise her."

"But there's something?"

Berto nodded. "Just… let me say this. They knew each other at school." He held up his hands. "I've said nothing, okay? I kept my promise."

Finn felt frustrated. Berto clearly knew something else, but he respected him for not breaking his oath. It gave him somewhere to start.

Throughout the day, Berto kept doing his impression of the KennaSpider, making Finn laugh and it lifted his mood. Aiden studiously ignored everything, just remained at his station.

After service, he left without saying goodbye to Finn. Clyde nudged Finn's shoulder.

"Trouble at home?"

"Just a blip. We'll be okay."

After the kitchen was closed up and clean, and the staff had gone, Finn went upstairs to the office. He'd cleared out Kenna's stuff the day he had fired her, and Aiden had taken it to wherever she was now. Finn didn't ask where.

So now, he rearranged the office to eliminate any memory of Kenna. He dumped her already-dying plants in the trash and took down the clichéd motivational prints she had framed and put up. Finn liked the looks of the bare walls—a new beginning.

Without telling Aiden, he'd even consulted a lawyer, just to check that he was within his rights to sack her. The lawyer assured him he was fine. "You have the proof of her bringing drugs into your home, aside from everything else. I wouldn't worry."

When Finn got home, the apartment was empty. Was Aiden with Kenna right now? Had he really taken her side that much? Or maybe he was there for the drugs…

*Fuck.* Finn grabbed his jacket and went out, finally finding himself back at the diner where he'd met Olly. It was an automatic thing for him to go into the café and order some fries and coffee. He'd been doing it every Tuesday for weeks now. After Olly got off work, he would come to join him and they would talk, about everything and nothing—work, music, movies, books. Nothing uber-personal, but then again, they didn't shy away from it either. Finn had told him he was still with Aiden and Olly was respectful of that, but their friendship was beginning to feel like something more was being forged, something special, without them giving it a name.

Tonight, Finn ordered his usual and went to find a booth at the back of the place. It was always quiet at this time of night and he found himself able to do what he loved—scouring the Internet for inspiration. He kept a notebook in which he scribbled down ideas for recipes as he scrolled through endless pages on *Instagram, Pinterest* and many other sites. He was careful now, given the experience with Kenna, that he never copied any of the recipes; rather he just let the ideas come to him, reading what other chefs were conjuring up.

Olly was late tonight. At two a.m., Finn was about to give up, thinking maybe Olly had gotten called out to a fire when the door of the diner opened. Olly's smile was wide and apologetic. "Hey, I'm sorry, man."

"It's no problem." Finn's heart was beating a little too fast, and he didn't want to think about why he felt a rush of joy when he saw Olly's face. *It's okay. You're not cheating. You're just friends.*

But when Olly shrugged out of his jacket, Finn couldn't help gaze at his broad shoulders in that grey marl t-shirt, the fabric stretched over Olly's well-formed pecs. Finn shifted his gaze away as Olly smiled at him. Finn could feel his face burn and cussed quietly to himself.

Olly didn't mention his red face, thankfully, and they chatted easily as they always did. Aggie brought over some fries and a refill of coffee for them.

"Usual, fellas?"

They thanked her and it wasn't until she moved back to the kitchen that Finn saw him.

His heart plummeted through the floor. No… no, it was impossible. The man was hunched over in his seat at the counter, his head turned away from Finn, but the jawline, the shape of his head, the way he slumped as if he were already defeated…

"Hey, Finn, you okay?"

Finn blinked back and focused on Olly. "Yes, sure, I just…"

The man at the bar slid from his seat and lurched to the door, disappearing out into the night. Finn stared at his retreating figure out on the street, then he looked back at Olly, his mind clearing.

"Actually… no. I'm not okay. Not at all."

Olly leaned forward and covered Finn's hand with his, his eyes kind. "Then why don't you tell me about it?"

* * *

There was a murmur of conversation that Finn picked up on as he entered his apartment and at first, he thought it was the television. Automatically, he ran through a dozen answers to the question "Where have you been?" so sure he was that Aiden would ask tonight, of all nights.

He hasn't yet, Finn reminded himself, then realized the voices weren't coming from the living room. He nudged the door to his and Aiden's bedroom open and peeked inside. Empty.

His adrenaline surged, along with his anger. He stalked to the end of the hall and threw open the door to the guest room, but even so, he wasn't prepared for what he saw. Aiden was naked, sprawled on his back on the bed and from the look on his face, high as fuck. His cock was ramrod hard, and Kenna's mouth was wrapped around it, moving up and down. Her eyes flicked up and met Finn's and her mouth curved up in a grin even as she sucked. There was triumph in her eyes.

Finn's body was ice, his mind still. He watched for another beat, saw that Aiden was completely out of it, and turned. He went to his bedroom, grabbed a bag from the closet. He dumped as many of his clothes would fit into it, along with his roll of chef's knives and his toiletries. In five minutes, he was out of the apartment.

No emotion would come. He grabbed a cab to Castro Hill and went to the restaurant. In the bar, he snagged a bottle of scotch from the bar and headed upstairs.

Finn dumped his bag on the floor and sat down, finally letting himself feel the shock of what had happened.

*Is it a shock, though? Really?* He realized that he had almost been expecting something like this for weeks now. Aiden wasn't Aiden—that succubus had leeched out any part of his boyfriend that he recognized. *Sucked it out*, Finn chuckled to himself then choked on the laugh.

Finn tested his heart and found it only a little broken. *No.* It was anger, he felt, rage. That little bitch had destroyed enough lives—he would not give her the satisfaction of destroying his.

He pulled out a drawer on the desk and found a legal pad and pen. Cracking open the scotch, and instead of crying, Finn Mason made a list of what he was going to do next, and at the top of that list, he wrote one word.

Win.

# Chapter Twenty-Three

Despite emptying almost a whole bottle of scotch, Finn was up before six the next morning and calling Aiden's father in New York. He saved Aiden the ignominy of telling his father exactly what had happened but just told Glenn Fox that the relationship had broken down. "Obviously, you'll want what's best for him and so I'm calling to work out how I can buy you out of the restaurant. I've—we've—built something here, but I understand if you want us to close, recoup your investment. I don't have the resources to buy you out. I have a small nest egg but nothing like you would need."

Glenn didn't hesitate. "Is he back on drugs?"

Finn wavered, then sighed. "I can't say for sure. But it looks like it, yes."

A long silence. "Give me the morning, Finn, and I'll call you back."

"Sure thing."

Finn showered in the small bathroom and changed his clothes. He would have to find an apartment—he couldn't afford a hotel for more than a few days and there was no way, *no way*, he was going to one of the cockroach motels out on the interstate. Even thinking about it, the smell of smoke seemed to fill his nose and the scars on his chest ached.

He did a cursory search for apartments but his heart wasn't in it. He could stay here for as long as he needed and at least it would save him the commute to work.

He went down to the kitchen now and, although it was already spotless, he spent the rest of the morning scrubbing every surface, sharpening his knives, and preparing his *mise-en-place* for the evening's service.

Glenn Fox called back after lunch. "I've spoken to my lawyers, Finn. The restaurant is yours. The papers will be with you by the end of the week."

Finn was staggered. "Mr. Fox…"

"Glenn."

"Glenn… this is too much. At least let me pay you back by instalments."

"Finn, without you, I would have lost my son years ago. You loved him; you saved him. You've given years to keeping him stable. I don't know the full story, obviously, but I can guess. Aiden is a grown man. He needs to take responsibility for his actions."

Finn couldn't work after that. He sat in the empty restaurant, listening to the sounds of Castro Hill outside and drinking soda. The weight of what had happened was finally hitting him and when, two hours before service, the door opened and Aiden walked in, all Finn felt was a deep sorrow.

Aiden stared at him for a moment, then went to snag a soda for himself. He brought a fresh one to the table for Finn and sat down, sliding the can over to him.

"Thanks." Finn studied him, wondering when it was that Aiden had switched. When he'd become her puppet. Aiden didn't meet his eyes for a long time and when he did, they were full of pain. He looked godawful, his blonde hair lank and greasy, his eyes bloodshot, dark shadows underneath them. Aiden looked sweaty and exhausted. He shook his head.

"I don't even know where to begin."

Finn crumpled his empty soda can. "Well, there's the drug use, or the blow job. Which one came first?"

Aiden winced. "I was out of it, I admit, I fell off the wagon."

"She pushed you off it. *Jesus,* Aiden. Correct me if I'm wrong but I was under the impression that you were gay. Was I wrong? All this time?"

"*She* started sucking *me.*"

"And you didn't stop her."

Aiden sighed. "No, I didn't."

"Did you fuck her?" Finn wasn't sure he wanted to know and felt a rush of nausea when Aiden nodded.

"I did. I'm sorry." A sly look came into his eyes then. "But you've been seeing that fireman."

*Ah.* "I've been talking to him as a friend, yes."

Aiden snorted. "Do you really expect me to believe—"

"—Yes, actually I do. I do expect you to know that I would never cheat on you." Finn's voice was like ice. "Because whatever arguments we have, however long we ignore each other, you should know that I loved you."

Aiden went very still. *"Loved."* He gave a humourless chuckle. "Past tense." His voice cracked and so did Finn's reserve.

"Love. I *love* you," he said softly, "you know that, right?"

Aiden just shook his head, then passed a hand over his eyes and Finn was shocked to see his tears. "I've fucked this up."

Finn was silent for a while, letting him get a hold on his emotions. "I just need to know… why *her*? Why have you been defending her? Is it because you wanted to fuck her?"

"No!" Aiden's shout made Finn start and Aiden held up his hands in apology. "No, of course not. I only ever wanted you."

"Then why?"

Aiden looked despairing. "I wish I knew. She… she's had it hard. When you threw her out, when you fired her…"

Finn's lip curled. "Ah, here comes the gaslighting. She teach you that too?"

"You never used to be this hard-nosed. She's just a kid and yet you think she's capable of what, exactly? Since we've known her you suspected her of throwing Lisa off of the Golden Gate, setting John on fire… what else?"

"I seem to recall she gave you the heebs when we first met her. And now *I'm* the paranoid one? I've talked to people, Aiden, I know things about Kenna Mitchell that would make you sick. Or not, apparently."

"You've been checking up on her?"

"Oh, yes." Finn, to his consternation, was starting to enjoy himself now. "Did you know she virtually persuaded a young kid to commit suicide?"

"Can you prove it?"

"No-one can say for sure. He was gay. She set her sights on him, shattered his relationship. Sound familiar?"

Aiden looked uncomfortable now. "We both know people like that."

Finn sighed. "I'm sick of being told I'm paranoid, that I'm victimising that little bitch. You know what love is, Aiden? It's having my back against everyone else. *Everyone.* Yes, honey, I love you… it's just a shame you don't know what that means."

"Don't say that." Aiden's voice was a whisper now and Finn could tell he was close to the edge.

"Go home, Aiden. We can manage service without you tonight. Get yourself together and we'll talk in the morning."

He half-expected Aiden to argue but he didn't, just shambled to his feet. He looked as if he'd aged a hundred years. He began to walk away, but then turned and pulled Finn into his arms. Finn didn't struggle, just let Aiden hold him for as long as he needed. Finally, Aiden stepped back and looked at him with bottomless grief in his eyes.

"I'm sorry, K.B. I really am."

It was the 'K.B.' that finally broke Finn as Aiden turned and walked away.

# Chapter Twenty-Four

If any of his crew noticed his red and puffy eyes at that night's service, they didn't mention it. But Finn was grateful for every comforting hand on the shoulder they gave him as they passed by. The restaurant was booked solid, a queue of people out of the door, so when Finn saw Sarah, the hostess, in the kitchen, he looked at her in surprise. "What is it?"

Sarah looked anxious; her eyes cloudy with trepidation.

"She must have booked under a different name, I'm so sorry, Finn. She said if I didn't seat her, she'd make a fuss, right there where everyone could see her."

Finn's heart sank. *Kenna.* He wiped his hands and followed Sarah back into the front of the restaurant. Sure enough, Kenna was sitting at the table in the window. She sipped her glass of water and regarded Finn coolly as he stalked over to her table.

"Don't even bother, Finn. I'm a paying customer, meeting a friend for lunch."

"Aiden isn't here," Finn said shortly, "and he's certainly not on the menu. I would have thought this place's 'chi' was all wrong for you."

Kenna smirked. "I can stand it for an hour. The person I'm meeting will be impressed with the place, I'm sure."

A hint of something crept into Finn's mind, a niggling doubt, a scintilla of dread.

"Look, Kenna. I think it's best if you leave. Right *now.* I don't want to make a fuss in front of my customers, but I will. All I'd have to do is tell them I was throwing out the woman who had her mouth around my boyfriend's cock last night—I'm sure they'd understand."

Kenna muttered something to herself and chuckled. Finn's eyes narrowed.

"What the hell did you say?"

She looked up slowly, gazing at him through her false lashes, not a hint of warmth in her eyes.

"I said, not just last night. Fuck, I never took you as stupid. We've been screwing for *months.*"

Finn's ears were ringing, the rush of blood in his head almost unbearable. *She's lying.* He stared at her, watching as her gaze shifted and she stood, smiling, simpering.

"Oh, and here's my guest. I think you know each other."

Somehow, he knew, he had always known, who he would see as he turned around. This wasn't how he wanted it to happen, not with a restaurant full of people watching them, but now it seemed inevitable.

Finn braced himself as he moved to confirm who the newcomer was. Jack Boyd smiled at him, nervous and trembling.

"Hello, Finn. It's been a while."

* * *

Aiden listened to his father rant and let it all wash over him. He'd heard this speech before so many times, but he had thought he never would again. He couldn't blame Finn for calling his dad, and when he heard that Finn had been willing to give up the restaurant, he knew for sure that their relationship was over, that he'd hurt him beyond measure.

And that was the thing that was killing him. *His K.B.* He should have listened to him, reassured him that Kenna was nothing more than a minor irritant.

He certainly shouldn't have been sleeping with her for all these weeks. What the hell had he been thinking? He'd done it for the pills of course. One Vicodin, every day, was all. His back ached from the long nights in the kitchens and it helped him relax—what was so wrong with that?

Everything. It had cost him *everything.*

Now he listened to his father and couldn't even muster an excuse. "Dad, look, do what you want. Just leave me to sort out my relationship on my own."

He ended the call with Glenn still in mid-rant and threw the phone down on the coffee table. *Jesus, what a fucking mess.* His head felt muzzy from the drugs and the tears that had come as soon as he realized what he had done.

Aiden hadn't taken it out on Kenna—how could he? It had been his choice to sleep with her, regardless of whether she manipulated him into it or not. And... she held a fascination for him. The sheer lack of empathy for others, the fact that she simply did not care if people thought she was bad. She was rotten to her core. He knew that. And yet...

His phone buzzed, and he picked it up unthinking. An image. Finn in the restaurant, talking to a man in his forties with half of his face a mess of scars. Aiden recognized that kind of scar. Burns, the same as on Finn's chest. Jack Boyd had come to town.

A myriad of emotions flooded through him. Panic, the need to go there, protect Finn from psycho Jack… but then he stopped himself. Would Finn really want his support? Wasn't he now just as bad as Jack? Okay, so, he hadn't tried to kill him, but he'd fucked Finn over just the same.

He heard the front door open and remembered too late that he'd given Kenna a spare key to the place one night when he was pissed with Finn. He always seemed to be pissed at Finn lately. He guessed it was guilt.

Kenna walked in. He could see she was high from the bright, excited look in her eyes.

"You get the photo?"

"I did."

Kenna flopped down on the sofa next to him, her hand immediately going to his thigh. She leaned over for a kiss—Aiden pecked her mouth quickly, mostly to keep her happy. She slid her hand up his leg and cupped his groin.

"Who is he?"

"The guy in the photo? I think it's Finn's ex-boyfriend."

"Hmm." Kenna kissed his ear. "They seemed to be having a pretty intense conversation when I left. Maybe there's still something there."

"Hardly." He didn't feel like explaining Finn's history with Jack to Kenna. Why was it that he felt like it would only be giving her more ammunition?

Finn's paranoia was catching, clearly. He got off the couch. "Come on."

"Where are we going?"

"Your place. It was a mistake to come back here last night. Finn deserves better."

Kenna got up and came to him. "So do you."

"I used to think so," he said sadly. "But now I'm not so sure."

* * *

Jack waited at the bar all night for Finn to finish up. Finn moved through service like an automaton and now, as his crew, casting curious glances at the stranger at the bar, left him alone, he steeled himself.

He walked out to the bar, feeling like that dumb, naïve kid from Whitewater again, instead of the successful mature restaurant owner he was. Jack looked as tired as Finn felt in his bones, but he had sat quietly at the bar, eating the food sent out for him and drinking only soda.

Finn grabbed a cold can from the fridge and motioned for Jack to join him at the table. "You still hungry?"

"Not at all. Your food is incredible. You went beyond anything I could have taught you. You're no small-town fry cook, Finn."

Finn gave him a wintry smile. "Thank you. Jack… What the hell are you doing here?"

Jack drew in a deep breath. "I wanted to know that you were okay. I needed to know."

"Why? Why now, after all this time? And, I might remind you, there is still a restraining order."

"I know, and I'm sorry." Jack looked at him earnestly. "It's selfish, I know, but I needed closure."

Finn said nothing for a while, just studied him. Then he sighed. "Jack, I don't know about closure, but I will tell you one thing. Stay away from Kenna Mitchell."

Jack's eyebrows shot up. "Why? She's seems okay. She's worried about you."

Finn laughed but there was no humour in the sound. "*Right.* I fired her and threw her out of mine and Aiden's home, but she's worried about me?"

"Is that so wrong?"

"Nope, Jack, it's not wrong, it's just not true. Kenna wants to paint me as some neurotic asshole who's losing it. This is what she does. She finds her mark, moves in, causes maximum destruction and is gone. She gets off on it."

Jack stared at him. "Wow."

"Can I ask you something?"

"Go for it."

Finn smiled at him now, even though his heart was going nine-to-the-dozen. Jack was no threat. Not now. All he was now was a sad, pathetic middle-aged man who had been used as a pawn.

"When did Kenna get in touch with you?"

Jack told him and Finn nodded. "Before my mom died… I was in Whitewater when someone followed me back to my hotel. A man. He met up with a girl… that was you and Kenna, right?"

Jack looked sick. "Yes. She told me… god, I'm an idiot."

"What did she tell you?"

Jack's whole body seemed to fold in on itself in front of Finn. "She told me… *man.* She told me you had never gotten over me, that you were struggling with your job, with your relationship. That you needed me. And, goddamn it, my ego told me she was right. I *wanted* to believe her."

He rubbed his eyes and then sunk his face into his hands. Finn got up and grabbed a bottle of Lagavulin from behind the bar. He put a heavy-based glass in front of Jack and poured two fingers of the scotch into it. "Drink, Jack. Take a breath."

He poured a finger into his own glass and knocked it back. Jack followed suit, nodding gratefully at Finn. "I was going to go to the hotel to see you, but then I heard your mom died. I'm sorry." He put his hand over Finn's.

Finn jerked his hand away. "Stop."

Jack sat back, shaking his head. "I'm sorry, I didn't mean…"

"You don't get to touch me like we're old friends, Jack. You tried to kill me."

"I know. Finn, please understand, I was crazy back then. Crazy about you. I couldn't even begin to think of what life would be without you."

"That's not love," Finn snapped back at him, the long-buried anger inside him beginning to roil and rage, "that's obsession. It's sick. Do you think I just walked away afterward? You went to jail, and I just got on with life? No, Jack. I was fucked in the head." He gave a humourless laugh. "Maybe I still am. And you coming here…"

"You seem to be doing okay." Jack looked around the now-empty restaurant. "And you landed on your feet with your boyfriend. I hear his dad funded this place."

Finn felt his anger burning in his chest. "Yeah, I landed on my feet with Aiden. Aiden, who, by the way, is probably fucking your friend Kenna right now."

Jack's eyes widened with shock, a first, then as Finn studied him, he saw a sly resolution creep into them. Jesus… he still thought he had a chance with him?

Finn pushed away from the table. "Jack, you came here, we talked and now I'd like you to go."

Jack nodded, slowly standing. "Can we have coffee some time?"

"No, I don't think that's a good idea."

"But if you're having problems with Aiden, you might need a friend."

Finn stared at the man in front of him, astounded by the man's delusions. He wasn't afraid—this version of Jack wasn't capable of hurting him now—he was just sad.

And *mad*. "If I need a friend, I'll go to someone who's never tried to kill me. Who didn't groom me from a fifteen-year-old."

"I never—" But Jack couldn't finish what he started saying. His shoulders slumped, and he nodded. "I could not help myself. You were the most beautiful boy I had ever seen and I… I should have been the responsible one. The decent man. But I never could be. I'm sorry, Finn, I mean it." He nodded at the empty glasses. "And thanks for talking to me, at least. It's more than I deserve."

Finn opened the door to the restaurant and Jack went out onto the street. He turned as if to say something more, but then, he just gave Finn a half-smile, a nod, and walked away.

Finn watched him disappear down to the tram exchange at the

end of the street. He tested his heart and found no sympathy there. Not for Jack. Not for Aiden. Not for himself.

The only thing there was anger. Fury. Finn went back in and grabbed his jacket, locking the door behind him. He hailed a cab—he wasn't risking running into Jack again on a tram—and while he rode into the city, he tapped out a furious text message.

When he got to the diner, Olly was already there. Finn's anger hadn't faded at all on the ride over, and he barely grunted a greeting at the man sitting opposite him.

"Hey, kiddo, how—"

"Fine."

Olly blinked. "Woah. Say it like you mean it."

Finn was too riled up to apologise. "Maybe this was a bad idea. I'm not exactly in the mood for a chat."

"Well, if that's what you want, buddy. Or we can just sit here and eat French fries and you can seethe in peace."

Finn's mouth hitched up at the corner, but he didn't want Olly to make him laugh or know that he nearly did. He wanted this anger, wanted this fire because it was cathartic. "Fine."

Olly smirked and called Aggie over. "Hey, you got a fuck ton of fries ready?"

Aggie was shooting Finn a worried glance and just nodded. "Coffee?"

"Yes, please."

"Thanks." Finn sounded more grudging than he meant to, but he shot Aggie an apologetic smile. She patted his shoulder as she went back to order their food.

Olly grinned at Finn and picked up a breadstick from the basket

Aggie had brought over and broke bits off, shoving them into his mouth with abandon. Finn did smile then.

"Hungry?"

"Pulled a double shift. Got off a half-hour ago."

"Oh, jeez, Olly, you should have said."

"No trouble. You sounded like you needed a friend."

Finn sighed. "Still. You must be exhausted."

"More hungry than anything. And anyhoo, I wanted to see you." His dark eyes were steady and for a second, Finn gazed back. Then his breath caught in his throat and he looked away.

"Hell, Olly… don't look at me like that."

Olly grinned broadly, his eyes crinkling at the corners. "Like what?"

"Like you…"

Olly didn't let him finish. He grabbed Finn's shirt and pulled him close, his lips finding his hungrily. The kiss was brief, sweet, and it sent thrills through Finn's tired body, soothing his fractured mind.

Olly let him go and sat back, grinning widely, almost smugly. "Now we've gotten that out of the way…"

Finn couldn't help himself: he started to laugh at the cheekiness of Olly's smile. "Man, that was risky."

"You're worth it."

Finn's chest tightened, and he looked away from Olly's gaze. "You can't know that."

"Yeah, I'm pretty sure."

Although Finn so desperately wanted to believe him, this sexy, confident man in front of him, he shook his head. "I can't do this. Not yet. I have to resolve what's happening between me and Aiden."

"I get it." Olly shrugged. "Look, Finn, I just set my stall out, is all. I like you. I think we've got somethin'. But, yeah, stuff is a mess at the moment for you. So… I'll wait. Until you say yay or nay. Whatever your answer is, you got a friend, okay? Someone who will always pick up your call. I got your back, buddy."

Finn didn't go back to the apartment that night. He didn't go home with Olly either, although he was tempted to more than he liked to admit. But he wasn't going to be that guy. He wasn't going to be Aiden. Just because Aiden had cheated, it didn't mean Finn had to get revenge.

But seeing Olly had shown Finn one thing.

There was hope for a future. Whether it was with Olly or not, that didn't matter so much as the resolve that now Finn knew what he had to do. The idea of not being with Aiden had been his worst nightmare. Now, it was the key to his own freedom.

Some things weren't meant to last forever.

# Chapter Twenty-Five

It was raining. A deep fog had rolled in from the Bay this morning, so thick the visibility was virtually zero, and when Finn looked out of the window of the apartment all he could see was a bank of grey nothingness.

It seemed apt.

The only sound was the occasional rustle as Aiden silently read through the papers Finn had his attorney draw up the previous week. It was the first time Finn had been back to the apartment for a week, buying fresh underwear and clothes instead of collecting his things. Now, though, his suitcase sat packed with the rest of his stuff near the doorway, Aiden casting sad glances at it. A box of Finn's cookery books and some knick-knacks Hannah had given him was next to the case. His world in still life.

But Finn couldn't feel sad. This apartment stunk of Kenna, her too-sweet, cloying perfume. Her supposed victory. Finn's jaw set. *Nope. You don't get to win, bitch.*

"You've been fair, considering."

He looked over at Aiden. His now *ex*-lover had at least showered and shaved. He hadn't seen him for days—Aiden hadn't shown up for his shifts at the restaurant and Finn, not stressing, had hired another chef and promoted Berto to be his sous chef. He hated to be pleased that Aiden's absence had barely impacted the restaurant in any way, but there was a smug satisfaction to it.

However, now, seeing the heartbreak in Aiden's eyes and knowing that this was it, the ending of their love, Finn could feel nothing but sorrow. Aiden straightened the papers up, then scribbled his name where Finn's attorney had indicated.

"Dad said he'd given you the restaurant and the apartment. I couldn't blame him."

"You should have the apartment. That way we can both have something to build on."

Aiden handed him the wad of papers, but as Finn took them, Aiden grabbed his hand. "K.B… I'm sorry. I fucked up royally."

Finn felt his throat constrict and gently, he withdrew his hand. "I know. Me too. I should have… I should have… god, I don't know, Aiden." His shoulders slumped, and he sat down heavily on one of the breakfast bar stools. He studied Aiden now, and the two men stared at each other as if trying to figure out what the hell had happened. "We made it," Finn said, quietly. "We actually made it, realized our dream, and then we blew it."

"*I* blew it, K.B. – and it was always *your* dream, your passion that got us here." Aiden got up and came to him, and Finn didn't pull away this time. Aiden kissed him softly. "You, Finn Mason, are the love of my life and…"

They were interrupted by the intercom buzzing. "*Shit.*" Aiden hissed and went to answer it. "Yeah, hello?"

"Finn Mason?"

"He's here, who is this?"

"SFPD. We'd like to talk to Mr. Mason, please."

Aiden buzzed them in. Finn was still thinking about what Aiden had said. Could he really leave him? Was there any way to forgive what had happened? The kiss had thrown him into turmoil again.

If only it hadn't been her… why did it have to be her? Of anyone he could have cheated on me with, it had to be that psycho bitch…

"Finn Mason?"

Finn blinked back into the present and saw the police officer holding his hand out towards him. "Yeah, that's me." He shook the police officer's hand. "What can I do for you?"

"Mr. Mason, do you know a man called Jack Boyd?"

And then Finn knew. He felt the blood drain from his face. "Oh, Jesus…"

The police officer nodded. "I'm sorry. Yes, we found Mr. Boyd's body this morning at a motel out on the highway. There was a note, which is how we found you."

Finn's horror turned to numbness. "Do you need me to identify him?" The words came out before he could stop them, and he heard Aiden clear his throat. "I mean, he used to be married, and I think he has kids, so maybe…"

"I know it's a lot to ask but when we notified his family back in Kansas, they declined to travel out here. Apparently, they've been estranged since he went to prison. I'm afraid you're it."

Finn nodded. He felt the burn scars on his chest constrict and contract, tension and a bottomless sadness inside him. Had Jack killed himself because of Finn's new rejection of him?

No.

Finn was as sure as he could be that Jack would have known what his reaction would be. Maybe it had been his last hurrah, one last grasp at the rope. Finn couldn't blame him for trying, even it had been insane. Jack had been messed up long before he'd met him, Finn realized now. He was just the catalyst.

It still hurt.

"K.B., do you want me to come with you? You shouldn't be alone when you do this."

Finn hesitated then shook his head. "No, I—"

"What's going on?"

They all started as Kenna came into the room. No-one had heard the front door open. She dumped her bag on the chair and put her hands on her hips.

*Always performing.* Finn's lip curled, and he looked at the police officer. "Actually, Ms. Mitchell also knew Mr. Boyd. They've been friends since at least October. Perhaps you should ask her about the relationship they had."

"What the hell, Finn?" Aiden was frowning and Finn turned to him, smiling without humor.

"Did Kenna not tell you? She was in Whitewater with Jack when my mom was dying. Trying to get him to contact me, even then. She was the one meeting him at the restaurant last week." He tuned back to Kenna. "And now he's dead. Just like Lisa. Just like John. Just like that poor kid who jumped from the Golden Gate. And the common denominator here is…?"

"What's going on?" The police officer sounded confused and a little pissed off, but Finn didn't care. He met Kenna's gaze steadily.

"Come on, Kenna. This is your chance for the spotlight. Why did you bring Jack to San Francisco?"

"I have absolutely no idea who or what you're talking about."

"Well, it shouldn't be too hard to prove." Finn looked at the police officer. "You can look at airplane records, right? Her credit card receipts?"

"Finn, stop it. You're upset about Jack, that's all."

But Finn couldn't take his eyes off Kenna, and the knowing smirk that was playing around her mouth. "You little bitch. What did you say to him? What did you say to make Jack kill himself?"

"Okay, that's enough." The policeman beckoned. "Come with me, Mr. Mason. We'll talk more on the way to the morgue."

Finn brushed past Kenna, heard her little giggle. Why the fuck was he the only one to see what she was? To his satisfaction, however, just as he walked out of the apartment, he looked back to see Aiden staring at Kenna, his expression confused and wondering.

Yeah, baby, your little fuck buddy isn't who she says she is... and her façade is slipping.

* * *

No matter how much you fear or hate someone, seeing them dead is a primal, bone-deep horror. *I used to love you, or at least I thought it was love.* Finn stared down at Jack's body. His face, slack in death, the deep-etched lines under his eyes, the partially open mouth. The spattered blood that they had yet to clean from his body. Jack had opened his veins, the coroner told Finn gently, and he'd done it so there would be no chance of salvation.

"From the drugs and alcohol in his system, he made the decision and did it right away."

Finn couldn't stop looking at the body. "Or someone else did it to him."

"That's unlikely."

Finn blinked and looked at the medical examiner. "Why?"

"There were hesitation marks, the note, his fingerprints on the razor. Of course, there will be an investigation, but given all the circumstances, it's pretty much conclusive."

"Could someone have talked him into it?"

The police officer, who Finn remembered now was called Larry, shot Finn a warning glance. The coroner cleared his throat and looked uncomfortable. "I can't speak to that."

Finn nodded. "What happens now?"

"The formal autopsy, the report and then the city will release the body for the funeral."

Finn took a deep shaky breath in. "I… I'm not sure who… he has kids, grown kids. I'll try to get in touch with them."

"We can do that for you, Finn." Larry put his hand on Finn's shoulder. "Come on, I'll buy you a coffee."

They sat outside at the café down the block from the medical examiner's office. The coffee was hot and strong, but Finn still felt a deep, cold sadness inside him. Larry was studying him. "I looked into Jack Boyd's past, Finn. Maybe it was a mistake to ask you, of all people, to identify him."

"There was no-one else."

Larry nodded. "Yeah."

The rain had stopped, but the air was still full of a fine mizzle of dampness that penetrated Finn's clothes and clung to his skin.

"Look… if the family doesn't want his body, then, I'll arrange a burial. Jesus." He rubbed his face. "I can't believe I'm saying this. There was a restraining order, you know? The man tried to kill me and yet…"

"Love is a funny thing. Even when we think we hate, there has to be something tangible that makes us have that force of emotion."

"He was just a lonely sad man at the end," Finn said. "Look, I have to get back to work, but… can I ask you something?"

"Go for it."

Finn hesitated. "In your line of work," he began carefully, "you ever come across sociopaths?"

Larry laughed. "Yeah, quite a few."

"I know, dumb question. What I mean is, ever been fooled by one? So much so that, afterward, you wonder how you were ever taken in by them?"

Larry finished the last of his coffee. "You talking about that girl at your apartment?"

Finn nodded and Larry sighed. "Look, professionally, I'm not a psychologist. Nor can I officially look into your accusations without a good reason."

Finn felt a flicker of hope. "But…"

"What's her name?"

"Kenna Mitchell."

Larry nodded. "I'll look into what I can. If there's anything, I'll get back to you."

"I'd appreciate it." Finn stood to leave, saying goodbye to the man, but as he turned Larry called him back.

"Finn… don't take anything into your hands, you hear me? I

understand your anger, but channel it elsewhere. Understood?"

Finn nodded. "Understood."

Finn went back to the apartment, just to pick up his stuff, and found it outside the door. Clearly Kenna had demanded his belongings be moved out after the confrontation earlier. He shrugged, checking everything was there, then hoisting the box into his free arm, he dragged his suitcase down to the street. He looked up at the apartment where he had thought his future would be set. His love, his family, his future. It had all imploded so quickly.

Finn shook his head. *Time to grow up, Finn boy. Life ain't a fairy tale.* He turned away, and it wasn't until he'd hailed a cab and gotten in that he realized he'd left the legal paperwork at the apartment.

*Shit.* Well, he wasn't going to go back now. He'd call Aiden and have him messenger the papers to the restaurant. Finn gave the cab driver the restaurant address and sat back. Time to move on. His phone bleeped, and he pulled it out to find a message from Olly.

French fries 2nite? O.

Finn let out a deep breath, feeling his body relax. *Yeah,* he sent back, *that sounds just about perfect. See you then.*

* * *

Kenna watched Finn from the kitchen window as he got into the cab. Aiden had left the apartment a while ago. "I gotta take a walk."

He hadn't been able to meet her eyes. After Finn had left with the police, she'd asked him what had happened. Aiden had stared at her for a long moment. "Is it true?"

"Is what true?"

"Did you know Jack Boyd?"

She'd rolled her eyes. "As if. Why the hell would I know anything about Finn's ex-boyfriends, if that's who he was?"

"Finn said—"

"Oh, god, *Finn* said? At this point, why do you believe anything that comes out of his mouth? He's been fucking around on you for god knows how long with that fireman, and yet, you still trust him?"

Aiden had paled. "You have no evidence of that?"

"You're not that naïve, Aiden." She sat down and crossed her legs. "Even if he started seeing him *after* he caught you and me, he was technically still cheating."

Aiden shook his head and she could see he was conflicted. *Nope. No way.* She'd worked too hard for this for him to slip away now. She got up and went to him, pressing her body against his. "Baby, let's not fight. Finn's obviously upset about his friend. I feel for him, I do. That's why I'm not getting angry about his constant antagonism toward me."

She laid her head against his chest. "I'm tired, Aiden. Tired of having this man treating me like I'm some kind of parasite. He gave me the job, he invited me into your lives."

She allowed a couple of tears to snake down her face—a sacrifice as her highlighter was on *fleek*, today—but it did the trick. Aiden's arms went around her, and he held her tightly.

"It's okay, honey. Just a bad day. A bad day all around."

She'd thought his mood had softened but after a while, he'd slunk out of the apartment and she knew he was feeling guilty again. *Annoying.* He'd have to get over this soon or she'd lose patience with him, but there was no way she was going to do that before the game was done.

Before she'd won.

She watched Finn's cab pull away from the sidewalk. In her hand, the papers that gave him the restaurant, Aiden the apartment. Colors, red, orange, yellow, even blue, flickered as the paper seared and curled over the burner. She'd rolled the papers up so that she held a torch now, watching them burn. Aiden, the weak fool, had signed them, and Finn had left them behind. But she would swear blind he'd taken them and had forgotten. Finn would again get angry—all the better for her. There would be no evidence the papers were ever here.

She held the burning roll of papers until the flames almost licked her fingertips and dropped the remaining pieces into the sink. She had burned the envelope first. Now she washed the remnants down the drain and smiled grimly. She was so close.

Aiden would be persuaded to get the restaurant back—after all, his father was paying for it—and then she could plan her final moves.

Aiden had been easy, almost *too* easy to corrupt. She kept him pliable now, both with the coke she would share with him and her sex. He was weak and couldn't say no, but unbeknownst to him, Kenna had been changing out his Zoloft even before Finn moved out. It had made his mood destabilize, and that's when she had gotten to him.

Easy.

Finn… Finn was a different prospect, a challenge, and Kenna was relishing it. Jack Boyd had been an inspired idea, and if this didn't break Finn, then what she had planned next would.

She could hardly wait.

# Chapter Twenty-Six

Something was making him crazy. Finn looked around the kitchen just as service opened. *Mise-en-place* all done—Berto at his station, the rest of the staff ready to go. The restaurant was full. Front of house staff were all in, all waiting tables or serving drinks.

So, what the hell was bugging him? *Fuck it.* He shook his head and, as the ticket machine pumped out the orders, he called them out: "Berto, three duck, two lamb. Clyde, two salmon, one red snapper…"

The feeling stayed with him throughout the evening, and although he remained focused on the job, Finn felt the weight of whatever it was on his shoulders. Maybe it was just irritation. Aiden had insisted that he'd taken the paperwork for the transfers with him when he left that day. Finn knew he hadn't.

"Finn, I've looked everywhere. The papers are not here. How many different ways can I say it?"

They hadn't spoken since. Finn called his attorney and got him to send over copies to Aiden. Maybe it was the fact Aiden was dragging his feet with them now, after being so willing to sign them before. It didn't take a genius to work out who was behind that particular little power play, but Finn would keep sending copies until Aiden got tired of playing games. He wasn't worried about the legal side—Aiden's father had made it clear that he thought Finn was being overly generous giving the apartment to Aiden, but that it was his decision to make. "Just make sure he signs over the restaurant. It's yours, Finn. Make me proud. Hell… you already do, son."

That had hit Finn hard, but in the best way. It was something his own father had never said to him.

Despite his antsiness, service passed without a hitch and after he'd cleared up and his crew had said goodnight, he went upstairs. He had gotten tired of sleeping on the floor of the office and had a futon delivered a couple of days back, but now, it just looked like loneliness. This night, he didn't want to be alone.

Finn grabbed some things, shoving them into his jacket pockets, and headed out of the door. He knew the tram route to the diner by heart now, and as he walked towards the warm, friendly lights, he could already see Olly waiting for him.

There was a smug of soot on Olly's face. When he stood to greet him, Finn wiped it away before taking Olly by surprise and planting a kiss full on his mouth. The kiss went on for longer than either of them expected it to, and when they finally broke away, they both laughed as they heard Aggie give a cheer from the other end of the almost-empty diner.

"Well, that was *very* welcome," Olly said, and made to sit down but Finn shook his head, smiling.

"Feel like continuing it? Your place?"

Olly's eyes widened, and for a moment, Finn's bravado faltered.

Then Olly's grin widened, and he got up. "You got it, buddy. Hey, Aggie? Hold the coffee, darlin'. We got other plans."

Turned out Olly lived a couple of blocks from the diner, and they had to walk past the firehouse to get there. "Wanna go in, meet the gang?"

Finn raised his eyebrows but Olly grinned. "Just kidding. Come on. I got a fridge full of beer."

Olly's apartment was tiny, an open plan loft space—if something that small could be described as a 'loft'—but it was clean and warm, and the battered leather sofa was a hell of a lot more comfortable than the futon back at *Homefires.*

They sprawled about, chatting, watched some humorous videos on YouTube, and drank Olly's beer. Finn was glad there was no tension between them, no expectation, and when Olly kissed him again, it was the most natural thing in the world to tangle his fingers in his short hair and kiss him back.

Olly's bed, it turned out, was even more comfortable than his sofa. Finn had expected to be nervous, but Olly's easy-going manner and his effortless sensuality had him so chilled out that by the time Olly eased himself into him, Finn was lost in the moment, his body unfurling under his gentle touch.

It was dawn before they fell asleep, sated and happy. Olly looped his arm around Finn's waist, spooning into him as they slept and for the first time in months, Finn felt safe.

In the morning, Olly cooked eggs for their breakfast. "Now," he said, waving his spatula at Finn, "I don't want to hear any cheffy criticism. These eggs are my jam."

"Well jammed, chef, but they're burning."

Olly's head whipped around and Finn chuckled. "Gotcha."

"Jerk."

Olly's eggs were delicious, Finn had to admit—it didn't stop him teasing Olly throughout their meal. It was good to make this gorgeous man laugh.

Olly pushed his plate of eggs away. "So."

"So?"

Olly nodded at Finn's chest. "You going to tell me?"

So, Finn did. He told him about Jack, about what had happened all those years ago, about Kenna bringing him back into his life. About Jack's suicide. Olly shook his head. "*Man.*"

"Yup."

"And you actually identified his body? After everything?"

Finn nodded. "You know what? I stopped being angry with Jack a long time ago. He was just a sick guy, a vulnerable guy."

"Not as vulnerable as a fifteen-year-old kid, Finn. Call it what you will. He groomed you. So, fuck him." Olly was angry now and Finn held up his hands.

"I know, but he's dead, so…"

Olly nodded, fiddling with his napkin. "And this little… psycho. She's dangerous."

"Yup."

"If I were you, I'd play her at her own game."

Finn shrugged. "As far as I'm concerned, she's not my problem any more." He didn't know how much he believed that, but right at this moment, he didn't even want to talk about Kenna Mitchell.

"Hmm."

"What?"

Olly shook his head. "In my experience, people like her will want to continue the game through to its end."

"What end? She thinks she won. She got Aiden."

Olly snorted. "Forgive me, but it doesn't seem like *he* was the prize."

Finn went very still. "What do you mean?"

"You, Finn. You're the talent, the fire behind everything. Aiden was the passenger."

"No, that's not fair. Aiden was... *is*... a good man." But even as he said the words, he began to see it. The similarity between his relationships with Jack and Aiden. Both of them screwing up just as Finn was about to soar. Jack, with his clumsy murder/suicide attempt when Finn told him he was going to New York; Aiden screwing Kenna just as Finn's reputation in the restaurant world was beginning to gain traction.

And both of them had laid the blame for their screw-ups on him. The realization that he'd attracted them, had thought himself loved and *in* love...

"Oh, Jesus..." He buried his head in his hands.

Olly said nothing but got up and came to him, rubbing his back. Finn took a few deep breaths and then looked up, trying to smile. "You don't have any major hang ups, do ya?"

"Me, nah." Olly grinned. "I'm an open book. Also, dude, I'm a freaking fireman. I ain't no-one's sob story."

Finn laughed. "Well-played, sir."

Olly's smile faded. "Seriously, Finn... you're the star." He sighed and sat back. "But I get it. I'd want to protect my ex, even if he had dumped on me from a great height. Like I said, play her at her own game. Expose her by something other than just hearsay. Actual tangible truth that can't be disputed. She needs to be humiliated, publicly. Her name needs to be spread around so that her poison is ineffective."

An idea began to form in Finn's mind. "Huh."

"What?"

He looked at Olly and hesitated for a moment. Could he do this? Would Olly really support him… "You said I'm the star, right? The prize?"

Olly grinned, rubbing his back again. "Hell, yes."

"Then why don't I give her what she really wants?"

Olly's grin froze. "What?"

Finn gave him a grim smile. "I've been resisting and so she had to play the long game. She's already tried to seduce me—albeit in an amateurish way—but she knew she was getting nowhere. So, she honed in on Aiden. Let's see how quick she is to switch her affection to me."

He saw the uncertainty in Olly's eyes. "Hey… it's an act. I just want her out of Aiden's life too. Then he can go to hell for all I care."

"But you do care enough to do this for him."

Finn's jaw set. "She doesn't get to win. Anything. That's all I care about. Whether she did have something to do with the deaths, however, abstractly, Kenna Mitchell needs to be stopped. I think I can do it." He glanced back at Olly. "It won't mean anything."

"I know that. And I get why this is the only way. It's just… nah, I don't get to be jealous yet. Sorry."

Finn smiled at him. "You can be… a little. Just know it won't mean anything. You and me… I'd like to see where this goes."

Olly leaned in and pressed his lips against Finn's. "Me too, Chef. Me too. Now… you finished your breakfast?"

"Yup."

"Good. Because I'm taking your body back to my bed, Mason."

Finn laughed. "Marking your territory?"

"Fuck, yes. Now, move your fine ass…" Olly's smile was broad, seductive and amused.

Finn moved his fine ass.

# Chapter Twenty-Seven

In his head, Finn had come up with a name for his plan. *Operation All In.* He and Olly had discussed how to go about exposing Kenna, and the first thing they had agreed was that Finn needed to reconnect with Aiden as a friend.

"But don't go all saccharin on Kenna. If you start being all friendly with her, even give a hint of it, she'll know you're playing with her. Nope. Maintain the antagonism with her but try to build bridges with Aiden."

"Got it."

Olly looked at him. "You look determined. You got a way to get to her?"

"The club. The BDSM club."

"Woah."

Finn smiled. "It's the last place she'll expect me to be. It'll unsettle her. I won't stay long, just enough time for her to see me. Then I'll keep popping up in places she won't suspect. Act out of character." He grinned widely. "Cock block her, if you will."

"I like it. It's devious and sneaky and I'm here for it."

They both laughed. Olly took Finn's hand and kissed his

knuckles, feeling the rough skin of the chef who worked his kitchen hard. "Whatever you have to do."

"I know it's a lot to ask, and just know, it means nothing."

"Dude, I trust you. This bitch needs to go down."

Finn was surprised that he wasn't at all nervous about going to the BDSM club. He'd researched the club, *Deviance*, online when Greg had told him about it and it seemed like any other fetish club—nothing threatening, no scandals. He snickered to himself. *Because, Finn, you're so used to these places.* He didn't bother dressing up for the club: white tee and jeans would do, and the woman at the door greeted with a professional smile as he said hello. "Hi. Newbie?"

"Kind of."

"Well, enjoy. We're open-minded and non-aggressive, but you have any problems, come see me."

Finn wondered if she was as friendly with everyone, and when he saw her plaster the same smile on for the women behind him, he got his answer. That was the lay of the land then; friendly but strictly professional. There was something comforting about that.

The club's interior looked exactly how he remembered from Greg's photos. What the images hadn't captured was the slow and sensual pulse of the music and the charged atmosphere. The place smelled like sex.

Finn moved through the place, his eyes raking the clientele for Kenna, but never lingering too much on any one person. There were people kissing, chatting, laughing – even some having sex openly – but, Finn guessed the real business happened back in the private rooms. He guessed that's how the place made its money—

chalkboards with the prices for each room, designated by color, were everywhere.

He headed for the bar, and soon realized that the mark-up on the liquor was also a major income for the place. The bartender looked at him with interest. “Haven’t seen you before.”

“Just trying it.”

“Good for you.” He slid a drink over to Finn. “First one’s on the house.”

Finn smiled cautiously. The way the bartender was looking at him was flattering but he wasn’t interested. He was here for one reason—Kenna.

It was an hour before he heard her laugh from somewhere behind him. The sound of it made his neck prickle in revulsion, but he deliberately kept his expression blank as he turned to scan the room.

Kenna draped herself over a group of young men, most of whom seemed drunk or on their way. She wore little, and Finn’s nose wrinkled at the cheap leather harness she had strapped around her body. Her breasts, small and the nipples popped and erect, were crisscrossed by the straps, which swept under and between her legs. She wore panties, but they were of such fine mesh that nothing was left to the imagination. Finn watched as she helped herself to the boys’ champagne, then grabbed one of their hands and guided it between her legs. She laughed uproariously at the uncomfortable expression on the young man’s face, especially when his friends started to tease him.

Bitch.

Finn stared at her, his face grim, until she sensed his scrutiny and looked over. He felt a jolt of satisfaction when she registered his presence and her expression changed. Surprise. Shock. Discomfort.

Finn slowly and carefully raised his glass in greeting, never taking his eyes from her face. He was enjoying the fact that she was unnerved. He gave her a sarcastic smirk, and just as it looked like Kenna was about to come over, he slowly drained his drink, thanked the bartender, and walked out, not looking at her again.

Outside, he had expected her to follow him but when she didn't, he knew he'd gotten to her. *Yup, didn't expect to see me on your hunting ground, did you?*

One down. His next move would take more courage, he knew, but it had to be done. The only thing he would regret was that it meant putting Aiden in the crosshairs. Despite everything Finn knew, he didn't want Aiden to be hurt. He didn't want him back, not romantically, but there was history; there were good times to remember.

*You're too soft-hearted.* How many times had Aiden said those words to him? Well, maybe so, and now Finn knew that wasn't a bad thing, that it wasn't a weakness. What was a weakness was tolerating abusive behaviour and Finn was at the end of his tether with that, from everyone. *Jack, Aiden, Kenna.* Aiden, at least, was redeemable. Olly might argue, but it was still too early in their relationship for him to put his foot down. If it hadn't been for Aiden, there would be no *HomeFires* and Finn was determined to drag him out of the quagmire he was in one last time. He owed him that much.

Which is why, the next morning, when Finn walked along the sidewalk to his old apartment building, he quelled any doubts and pressed the intercom. Thankfully, it was a surprised Aiden who answered and buzzed him in.

Finn walked into his old home and it was like walking into the past. Without Kenna's presence, he could almost believe it was six months ago, except Aiden looked stressed out, and Finn had to be told to have a seat.

Fuck. How did it all come to this?

"How're you doing?"

Aiden looked up from the coffee pot he was holding. "Surprised to see you, but otherwise…"

His skin was pallid, and his hands shook. "You in withdrawal?"

"No need to sound so surprised. Yeah, figured I'd better get my act together."

Finn was more relieved than he showed. "Good job. Talking of which…"

Aiden frowned. He waved the coffee pot at Finn, who nodded. "Yes, please."

Aiden made the coffee automatically adding creamer and sweetener the way Finn liked it. He slid the mug to him.

"Thanks. Look, Aiden, I won't beat around the bush. I want you back… at the restaurant." He hadn't meant to pause, but something in him, a latent anger, felt the need to give Aiden hope and when he saw the spark of it die in Aiden's eyes as he added 'at the restaurant', Finn felt guilty. That was beneath him.

"Right. At the restaurant. I thought you'd found a sous chef?"

"We have and he's working out great. You… you couldn't come back as my second, you know that, right?"

Aiden sighed. "Yeah. I guess."

"Look, I'm just saying, if you need a job, it's there for you. I don't see why us splitting should impact your career, especially if you're back in NA."

Aiden's eyes narrowed. "Why? I fucking cheated on you and now you're Mr Peacemaker? What are you up to, Finn?"

"Exactly what I said. Your job, albeit changed, is there for you. We don't have to make this unpleasant."

"And Kenna?"

Finn steeled himself. "What about her?"

"You going to rehire her too? Are you that magnanimous?"

"*Fuck*, no. I don't want that spider anywhere near me or my business. Or *you*, for that matter but that's not my call. This is about trying to rescue our… friendship."

"Right." Aiden got up and dumped his coffee down the drain. "All while you're fucking that fire chief."

"Yes."

Aiden looked away from him, leaning on his hands and gripping the side of the sink. "*Jesus*, K.B."

Finn knew he hadn't expected that answer, but it was only fair. He was with Olly now.

"I'm sorry, Aiden, but…"

"… but I fucked Kenna and lost you. That's on me. But you sure moved on quick."

"I didn't, actually. I haven't." Finn could feel his resolve dissipating. "I miss you, and god damn it, yes, I still love you. But I'm not *in* love with you any more. I don't trust you. You know me well enough to know trust is the real deal breaker here. Olly… he's good for me and I hope, some day, to be good for him. I hope I can make it work. Doesn't mean I don't miss you every day."

Despite *everything*. But he wanted Aiden to at least know, if he wasn't forgiven, he was still… what? Maybe this had been a mistake. He didn't want to hurt Aiden, but maybe by holding on, that's exactly what he was doing.

Then Kenna stalked into the room and Finn forgot all about altruism. He and Kenna stared each other down. *I know what you are, girl. I know how you work.*

Kenna dropped her gaze first. She went to Aiden, slid an arm around his waist. Territorial pissings. Finn couldn't give a crap.

"What's he doing here?"

Finn saw Aiden carefully slide away from her touch. "It's just business."

"What business?" She narrowed her eyes at Finn. "That restaurant is morally half Aiden's."

Really? Okay, if she wanted combat, she'd get it. "But legally all *mine*. Nevertheless, there'll always be a job for Aiden there."

"If it lasts. Most restaurants close within a year." Kenna retrieved a dirty mug from the sink and rinsed it out. She nudged Aiden with it, nodding to the coffee pot. Two spots of pink appeared high on Aiden's cheeks and, to Finn's amusement, he ignored the obvious order. Kenna sighed and poured herself some coffee, then came to sit across from Finn, tucking her legs up prettily. Even now, she was more concerned with her own curated, pretentious aesthetic than she was that Finn was in her space. She sipped her coffee, her dark eyes darting between the two men. "Well… Aiden doesn't need your job."

"I don't believe I was asking for your opinion. Aiden and I can discuss things between us." He kept his voice level, adding in a wink to Aiden, just to annoy Kenna.

Kenna looked at Aiden. "I hope you're not considering this."

"I am. I need a job, Kenna. This place won't pay for itself."

Kenna's mouth opened a little. "But can't you see what he's doing?"

"Offering me a job?"

Finn was enjoying this. Kenna glared at him. "It's not a job. He's trying to drive a wedge between us."

Finn was openly smiling now. "By offering Aiden his old job back?"

"You *fucker*." Kenna hissed at him and Aiden moved quickly to step between them.

"Kenna, can you give us a moment? I want to talk to Finn."

"But I—"

"—please." Aiden sounded exhausted. Kenna got up and left the room, slamming the door behind her. Aiden slumped into the couch seat she had vacated and put his head into his hands.

After a moment, Finn got up and went to sit by his ex-lover. "Aiden." He put his hand on Aiden's back, grateful when he didn't shrug it off. "You deserve better than this."

"I really don't." Aiden gave a humorless snort. "This is my penance."

"Oh, god damn it. Don't you see? If you let her defeat you, she's won."

"For fuck's sake, Finn! Don't you see? It's this attitude that sets her off! It *gets* her off."

"I know that. But I didn't trigger this. It was always in her endgame."

"Christ, I don't know which of you is worse." Aiden got up,

paced the room. "I don't want your job."

"Up to you. It'll always be there for you."

Aiden stared at him unhappily. "Why? I fucking cheated on you. With Kenna, a woman, for chrissakes. Why the hell would you be so…" He sighed, shaking his head. "I think you should go, Finn. Just… let me think."

Finn stood. "Of course." He clapped his ex on the back, determined to keep up a calm front although he felt like crying at the hopelessness in Aiden. It was the same despair he had sensed in Jack that last day and it scared him.

As he turned to go, Aiden grabbed him and crushed his mouth against his. Finn could feel the tears on Aiden's cheeks. After the kiss, Aiden leaned his forehead against Finn's. "I'm sorry," he whispered now, his voice cracking. "You were the best thing that ever happened to me and I destroyed it."

Finn felt his emotions spill over. He gripped the back of Aiden's neck. "Promise me. Promise me you won't…"

He couldn't say the words, but Aiden got it. "I promise, K.B."

"No matter how bad it gets."

"No matter how bad."

Finn left Aiden standing in the middle of the living room and left the apartment. Downstairs, he wasn't surprised to see Kenna waiting for him. She blocked his exit. Finn sighed, looking at her as if she were an annoying bug. "Get out of my way, Kenna."

"Not until you talk to me."

"The adults have done talking now. There's nothing more for you to contribute." He stepped around her but knew she wasn't finished.

"You'll regret it if you tell him about the club."

And there it was. The threat. He turned to look at her, a smirk hovering around his lips. "Why the secret? You hardly, um, *shy* away from exposing yourself." Finn let his eyes travel up and down her body, a look of disgust on his face. "And what about your *Instagram* page?"

"What about it?"

"Your photos. Very... enlightening." He leaned closer, lowering his voice. "Especially the ones your old friend Greg gave me when he told me what you did to Brooks."

With satisfaction, he saw Kenna pale a little. "Who?"

"Don't bother lying, Kenna. We both know you drove that kid to suicide... question is, did you do the same to Lisa?"

Finn was chilled by the fact that Kenna didn't even try to look sorry. Instead she merely looked impatient.

"What about my Instagram page?"

Finn shook his head – innocent people had died, but she was still more concerned about her social media following! The revulsion he felt was almost overwhelming, but he didn't want to show his feelings to Kenna. Instead, he shrugged.

"Probably should have changed your password a bit more often."

God, he thought as he turned and walked out, that was beyond satisfying. Kenna had grabbed her phone even before he'd stopped talking, but he didn't wait to see her reaction.

All Finn knew, right now, was that he was winning.

# Chapter Twenty-Eight

His good mood infected the crew at service that evening, and it only improved when, just before they opened the restaurant's door, Aiden appeared. Finn grinned at him. "You okay?"

"Let's just say it was better for me to be out of the apartment."

But there was an amused gleam in his ex-boyfriend's eye that gave him hope that maybe Aiden would extricate himself from Kenna. Maybe he would make it after all.

Aiden stayed to chat for a while, but shook his head when Finn asked if he was staying to work. "Naw, man. Not tonight. I think I gotta head home and start… changing stuff."

"You'll be okay?"

Aiden gave him a sad smile. "Don't worry about me, K.B."

The restaurant quietened down as the night drew on, and by closing time, the kitchen had already been half-cleaned. The crew ate together then drifted away.

Olly called Finn to tell him he was having to work a double shift. So, instead of going home to Olly's apartment right away, Finn went up to the office to deal with the paperwork that had been stacking up.

He flicked on his laptop as he sorted through the mail, and, mostly for his own amusement, he queued up Kenna's Instagram page. He smirked when he realized she had taken down the images he'd uploaded the night before, but still the comments on her other posts referred to them. Finn knew she would be deleting them, but still, it was satisfying to see some of the more trolling comments on her carefully-curated photos.

One showed Kenna, looking coquettishly over her shoulder, clad in a cream-colored chunky-knit sweater, holding an orchid. Underneath were the usual sycophantic posts but as Finn scrolled down, he began to notice the troll comments.

**Joby4510:** **Hey, it's cute and everything, but I preferred those 'other' pics. More please!**

**PinkBanana62:** **Seriously? Gross. But then again, so were those pics.**

**LiamGreensDick:** **Sit on me.**

**YoungGoon43:** **Dem tiddies doh…**

**FionaCaroSF1989:** **Honestly, I came here to say that I was so disappointed in you for showing those photos**

**JWPoonHound Ittybittytittycommittee!**

They went on, getting more and more explicit, and trashing Kenna and each other with impunity. Even the most rabid of Kenna's fans (and Finn shook his head at their ferocious defense of their 'queen') couldn't compete with the sheer number of negative comments.

Did he feel guilty? Not for a minute. Had he committed a crime?

Possibly, but Finn wasn't dumb. He'd taken his laptop, sat outside his old apartment, and connected to Aiden's WIFI to post the photos Greg had given him and then dumped the old laptop. Let them try to prove he was behind it.

Finn smirked and shut down the computer, glancing at the clock. It was just after midnight. Olly had told him he wouldn't be back until four at the earliest. Finn tackled the brunt of the paperwork for an hour then went back down to the kitchen. Sleep was evading him tonight, and so he decided to make a batch of his famous truffle mac-and-cheese to take home to Olly.

Working in the kitchen at night was a strangely-relaxing experience. He opened the hatches that looked out over the main restaurant so he could see out to the street as he worked.

Castro Hill at night was quiet. Occasionally he would see people walk past, sometimes, even dance past, as did one of the regular homeless residents. Finn waved at her as she passed but the woman didn't notice. The changing traffic lights right outside the restaurants cast a multi-colored glow, and the quiet hum of the kitchen's freezers and refrigerators made for a chilled-out white noise for Finn to work to.

He chopped up green onions, garlic, truffle and three different kinds of cheeses for the sauce, then melted butter and oil in a pan. He threw in the onions and garlic, breathing in the aromatic fragrance. Damn, his whole mouth filled with saliva—that never left him, even though he cooked all these ingredients every day. Finn grinned to himself. Food was the one thing he could always rely on to make him feel grounded and peaceful. Tonight's service had been fun, probably more light-hearted than it had been in weeks, maybe months.

When the sauce was made, he poured it into the macaroni and spread it into a baking pan, sprinkling the breadcrumbs and seasoning on top. He slid it into the oven and set the timer, checking his watch. Twenty-three minutes after two. He cleaned up his workstation and went to the walk-in cooler.

Something fell down behind him and he turned to check what it was. Finn never saw the small figure stepping out of the shadows until the heavy-bottomed pan was swung into the side of his head.

He staggered back, his eyes whirling in his head. A foot slammed into his stomach and he was down. Finn caught the glint of the lights outside catch the steel pan as it was swung upwards. He brought his hands up, but it was too late. There was a bright white light and an agonising pain. Then all was darkness.

# Chapter Twenty-Nine

Olly Roberts stretched out his big body as he changed into his civilian clothes at the firehouse. He loved his job, was born for it, but pulling a double shift in his thirties was a hell of a difference to when he'd first started out. Damn, even five years ago, it felt different.

Still, if it had to be done, then he sure as hell wouldn't ask his crew to do something he wouldn't do himself.

Now, of course, was the fact that he had someone to go home to. Even after such a short time, knowing he would see Finn when he got home from work, made him antsy to get there. Tonight, though, he knew Finn would be at the restaurant and so he'd texted him earlier, telling him he'd come pick him up. "Bring you a corsage," he joked, and Finn laughed.

"Dude, you want to see the epic mac-and-cheese I'm making for you. You won't need to eat for a week."

So, Olly said goodnight to his colleagues and jumped into his car. The nights, or rather mornings, were getting colder now, and the mist rolled in from the Bay, thick and soupy.

Castro was quiet as he pulled over to the curb outside *HomeFires*.

A homeless woman was standing outside the restaurant, gazing into the restaurant. She was dancing from foot to foot as Olly approached.

"Hey, girl, you doing okay?"

She turned to look at him. "All them bright lights. They dancing."

Olly smiled at her. "Dancing, huh?"

She pointed through the window. "*Dancing.*"

Olly followed her gaze and his heart turned to ice. The dancing lights flamed red, yellow, orange. "Jesus, no!"

His cry scared the old woman who ran off as Olly began to bang on the windows. "Finn! Finn!"

He knew better than to try to break the window—the influx of oxygen would draw the fire throughout the whole building. No, he would have to go to where the fire was—the kitchen. He ran around to the side entrance, already calling the emergency services. He barked his instructions down the phone even as he kicked at the back door. He knew it was risky but there was no way he was risking Finn being in there without trying.

His breath came in panicked gasps as he rammed the door, first with his feet, then his shoulders, ignoring the pain shooting through his body as the door refused to give. Finally, he felt it move and with one last run up, he managed to break the door open. He staggered back as the flames roared out at him, eating up the fresh oxygen hungrily.

Once inside, the rush of heat was intense. All the oxygen seemed to be sucked from his body and he dropped low to the ground. The noise was incredible—the entire kitchen was on fire.

The smoke was so thick and dense, Olly had to feel around with his hands. In his gut, he knew Finn was here, was unable to get himself out, and when he felt the solid form of a human leg on the floor, he knew he had found him.

"Finn! Finn, buddy, you have to wake up."

But the body was still, and the effort of shouting filled Olly's lungs with thick, acrid smoke. If he didn't preserve his oxygen, neither of them would make it out. He managed to get his arms under Finn's shoulders and began to drag him. Finn's chequered chef pants caught alight as they were almost at the door and Olly had to stop and put them out. The whole place stank of smoke and fat and, with his experience, Olly knew that the kitchen's cooking oil had been used as an accelerant.

*Fuck that,* he knew who was behind this. This was no accident. Finally dragging Finn's dead weight out into the alleyway, and huffing great lungfuls of air into his own bursting chest, Olly got his confirmation.

Finn's face was covered in blood, jagged, vicious wounds at his temple and on his forehead. His nose was broken, blood had streamed from it and was now drying and crusting around his mouth and chin. His eyes were closed.

Olly tried to switch into professional mode, but to see his new love like this—he wanted to throw up. A crowd had formed both in the alleyway and out on the street and he yelled at someone to please come and help him.

A group of young men ran over and together, they helped Olly move Finn along the street and into the nearest open business, a twenty-four-hour bodega.

The owner cleared some space on the floor, bringing Olly some water and paper towels. Outside, Olly could hear sirens, fire trucks, but he couldn't have cared less about the restaurant burning down—he wanted paramedics, an ambulance.

Because Finn... Finn was still, too still. Now, as Olly ran through the checks that he performed automatically on any victim of fire, had performed so many times, there was one thing he knew right away and it was the thing that terrified him most.

Finn was not breathing.

* * *

Aiden had gone to a liquor store after leaving *HomeFires* and bought a bottle of scotch. He meant it to be his last—not that he was suicidal—but tomorrow, he was heading to rehab. He would prove to Finn that he hadn't been a waste of his time, and whether or not, there was any future for them as a couple was beside the point. At least, that's what Aiden had told himself. But yes. Tonight, drown the sorrows. A last hurrah.

What was even better was... he didn't enjoy the alcohol. He sat at home, on his couch in the dark, sipping occasionally, but really, he could have just been downing plain water for all the pleasure it gave him.

Aiden had stretched out on the couch when he heard the front door open. He frowned—he had thought Kenna was already in bed—there had been a lump of... something... in the bed when he'd glanced in. Hell, he'd even crept around the damn apartment so he wouldn't wake her.

Still—he didn't want to talk to her, so he remained quiet, and heard her go into the bathroom, crank on the shower.

Huh. It was a little after four a.m. and she was taking a shower? Aiden shrugged. He knew she went out to that club in the city—yeah, he knew all about *Deviance*—and he couldn't have cared less. Aiden just wished he had the guts to throw her out on her ass, but he couldn't bring himself to do it. Even after everything, she still had some strange and uncomfortable hold on him.

He listened to her shower shut off and waited for her to leave the bathroom. After ten minutes, he got up and knocked softly on the door. "Are you okay?"

He pressed his ear to the door. Was she crying? "Ken—"

The door opened, and she stepped out, a towel wrapped around her, a bundle of her clothes wrapped in her hands. "I'm fine. I'm sorry I woke you."

"I was awake."

She flinched and Aiden wondered why. "What's—"

Then he caught a whiff of something. "What's that?"

"Nothing." She slipped past him and into the bedroom, closing the door behind her. Aiden stared after her, then shook his head. Her clothes stank of something acrid. Maybe they'd had some kind of weird shit smoke party at the club.

Whatever.

But he couldn't get the stench out of his nose and he opened the windows of the living room and lay down on the couch. He flicked the television on, turning the sound off, flipping through the channels to find something to watch.

When he got to the local news, he stopped, his heart racing, and sat up.

Oh, god, please no…

The flames licked the *HomeFires* sign as the camera panned in and everywhere, fire officers and first responders milled around. Thick black smoke poured out from the restaurant's shattered windows and the reporter on scene was jabbering back to the anchor – for a moment, Aiden had a hard time deciphering the words coming out of the T.V.

All he heard was arson, foul play and serious injuries.

And Finn's name.

Nonononononono…

Aiden made it to the bathroom before he threw up—just. He emptied the contents of his stomach down the toilet then sat, panting for oxygen. *Finn. The restaurant on fire. Destroyed.*

Aiden closed his eyes, picturing Finn burning. He could smell the black smoke, feel the heat of the inferno, hear the agonized screams of the man he still loved.

He could *smell* the smoke.

His eyes popped open and even without realizing it, he was running, bursting into the bedroom. His hands were around Kenna's throat pressing down as he screamed with unrelenting rage and terror.

"What did you do? *What did you do?*"

# Chapter Thirty

There was pain and then there was this. Nothing like before. The choking smoke was a cake waltz to this. Finn wanted to open his eyes, especially when he heard the distress of those around him. Some voices he recognized… Olly… Hannah… Berto and Clyde. Others, more professional, still sounding appalled.

*So… I'm fucked then.* That was the take-away from what they were saying. And that was only when he could make sense of their words. His head was a ball of searing pain. Luckily, he kept drifting into the darkness, but somehow he knew he couldn't go all the way in or there would be no coming back.

Not ever.

Finn opened his eyes a crack. *Nope. Big mistake.* The bright whiteness in the hospital room seared his eyeballs, and he groaned. He heard the scraping of metal against linoleum and a soft voice say his name.

Olly.

Finn reached out with his hand and felt Olly's big fingers linked into his. A second later, soft lips brushed his mouth. "Hey cutie."

Finn tried to speak but nothing would come out. He felt a straw being gently placed between his lips and drew on it, the water on his tinder-dry throat a relief. "Olly?"

"Hey, bud. You doing okay?"

"Um…"

Olly chuckled softly, but there was a tell-tale brittleness to it. Finn turned towards the sound and opened his eyes again. Still too bright but at least now he was looking at Olly. His lover wore a smile but his dark, kind eyes were troubled. He reached over and swept a cool hand over Finn's forehead.

"Don't try to speak too much, hun. The docs said you might be groggy for a while."

Finn nodded and winced. His head felt like it was in a vice. Slowly, he remembered why. "How long?"

Olly hesitated. "A week."

*Jesus.* He'd been unconscious for a *week*? Fuck… "Olly, the rest—"

"Don't worry about that now." Olly sighed. "Babe, the police… they're looking for Aiden and Kenna."

Finn stared back at him, not wanting to acknowledge what he was being told. *No.* He could believe Kenna. He *knew* it had been Kenna who attacked him. She'd had the jump on him, even if he was twice her size and she'd hit him with something hard. Tire iron, maybe? Maybe a heavy pan? Christ, who knew? Who cared? It was the hatred behind it that counted.

But not *Aiden*… Even after all of this, Aiden wouldn't hurt him. That, he couldn't bear.

The doctor came in then and the next hour was full of irritating and painful tests, made worse by the sight of his sister glowering at the medical staff every time Finn groaned.

Hannah was pale, her eyes shadowed with dark circles and her face pinched. Finn knew that expression well—grief. When the doctor had finished, Finn reached out to his sister who took his hand. "Damn, Finn, can't you stay away from these places?"

"Sorry, sis." He winced. "Can I sit up?" He directed this at the doctor, who nodded.

"But carefully, and—" he directed a glare at Hannah and Olly, "—I don't want him too stressed. Another hour at most then I want you to rest, Mr. Mason. Deal?"

"Deal."

The doctor and Olly helped Finn into a sitting position. Finn's head whirled a little, and the doctor saw his eyes flicker. "Light-headed?"

"Just a head rush."

"Hmm. Well, believe it or not, you were very lucky. We were worried about brain swelling and, certainly, you were out for a few days. But, despite how bad your injuries look and feel, there's no sign of any permanent injury… at the moment. The burns on your legs are superficial. You'll be with us a few more days to make sure." He smiled kindly at Finn. "You taking any of this in?"

"Some." Finn chuckled softly. "Just glad to still be here."

"Well. The police will want to talk to you, but not today. If you can keep water down, we'll give you a light meal later. Hungry?"

"Not at all."

The doctor gave him a grin then. "The kitchen staff will be glad to hear that. I don't think they were happy about having to feed a famous chef."

"Not famous, and I bet their food is great."

The doctor patted his leg. "Take it easy. I'll be back later to check on you."

Finn thanked him. When he was alone with Olly and Hannah, he tried to smile at them. "Stop looking so tense, loves. I'm okay."

"Do you remember any of it?"

Finn nodded, his smile fading. "Yeah. Got jumped, hit with something hard. Guess that much is obvious. Woke up once, smelled smoke. Last thing I knew." He sighed. "No-one else was hurt, though, right? You would have told me by now."

"No-one else, Boo." Hannah looked like she might cry. "Just you."

"And the police are looking for Kenna?" He couldn't say Aiden's name just yet. He would not believe that his ex had any hand in this. *Attempted murder.*

He saw Olly and Hannah exchange a glance and begged them silently not to go there. Hannah sat on the edge of Finn's bed. "They went to your old apartment, and it was abandoned. Door wide open, clothes missing from the closet. They took off the night of the fire."

"So, the police are onto Kenna? Who told them she was the one who attacked me?"

"Finn..."

"No." He cut them off with a violent movement of his hand. "Just her. Just Kenna."

Hannah gave a quick, short nod and he could tell she was annoyed, but so be it. He wasn't ready to hear anything else.

The police came to see him the next day. A plain-clothed detective with a stern face questioned him and Finn went over everything again and again, from when he'd hired Kenna, through Lisa's suicide, to the time Kenna had dropped her towel in the shower, to when he hired her. He managed to get through it all without mentioning Aiden once, but the detective, Pete Krona, wasn't messing around. "Mr. Mason, it's time to talk about Mr. Fox."

The questions never seemed to end.

When did you and Aiden meet?

How long did you live together?

His father financed your restaurant?

His father gave you the restaurant after the split?

How did Aiden react to that?

Do you know Mr Fox Senior is paying your medical bills?

Sometimes he asked the same question multiple times and Finn got annoyed. "I've already told you that."

"I'm still not convinced you're telling me the whole story, Mr. Mason." Krona sighed now, looking at his watch. "But my time is up. I don't want to wear you out."

*Too late*, Finn thought darkly, but he nodded. "Fine." His head pounded, and he clicked on the little pump that dealt out his pain meds.

Krona looked at him sympathetically. "Finn, I'm not here to make your life worse. But you must face the fact that an innocent man doesn't go on the run. We found enough forensic evidence at the apartment to tie Kenna Mitchell to the fire and, according to your own story, she's never been so sloppy before. There's no way Aiden would have missed it. If Aiden cared about you, why wouldn't he turn her in? Why go on the run with her?"

"You don't know her. She's a master of manipulation. She

persuaded a gay man, not a bisexual, a *gay* man to become her lover. I believe she convinced Lisa, Jack and that other guy to kill themselves because they had either too much information about her, or they ceased to be useful." Finn stopped, aware his voice was getting louder.

He sighed, rubbed his aching head. "I need to rest now."

"Of course. I'll be back as soon as I have some news." Krona got up and went to the door. "Finn… sometimes people get into things they can't see a way out of. Doesn't mean they don't have to pay for their actions. At the very least, he's an accessory."

When he was gone, Finn asked Hannah and Olly if they could give him a few minutes alone. "You must be tired and hungry, guys. Please, go find yourself some food at the very least."

It took some persuasion but finally, they left him alone, Hannah with a glare that said "Don't do anything stupid"—as if he could, seconded to this hospital bed by the doctors. Olly gave him a soft kiss.

"I'll be back, cutie."

Finn smiled at him. This man didn't have to do this, didn't have to stay with him, put his life on hold for someone he barely knew.

Except… he *does* know me.

And so does Aiden…

When he was alone, he snagged his phone from the nightstand and found Aiden's number. He didn't hesitate to press call. He hadn't expected Aiden to pick up, so when it clicked to voicemail, he wasn't surprised.

"Aiden… it's K.B. That was a dumb thing to say – of course, you know it's me. I'm okay. A bit battered around, but I'm okay. Aiden…

I know you didn't do this. I don't know why you've decided to go with... Kenna. She did this to me, I don't have any doubt. Like I don't have any doubt she had something to do with Lisa, and John, and Jack. She's poison and she's going to get what's coming to her."

Finn sighed and closed his eyes. "Aiden... what happened to us? That's the worse part of this for me, the fact that we fell apart so fast. After everything we had built. Was it really a house of cards? It didn't feel like it."

He couldn't help the crack in his voice. "Why did we let her do this to us? We were stronger than that, weren't we?"

Finn couldn't help the sob that escaped him, and he held on while he steadied himself. His head throbbed, his eyes felt grainy and sore. He drew in a deep breath before he spoke again.

"The restaurant is gone. Our relationship is gone. *You*... are gone. But I'm still here. She didn't win against me, Aiden. Please... please, love... don't let her destroy your life any more than she has."

He sighed. "The police told me that they're going to charge you as an accessory. Turn yourself in, Aiden, don't make it worse. I'll... I'll speak up for you at the trial. Just please... stop running. There's nowhere to go from this."

God help him, he almost said 'I love you' but he couldn't. Because he didn't want that to be the reason Aiden turned himself in. Because it was manipulative, and Aiden had had enough of that from Kenna.

And because it was no longer true.

Finn finally ended the call, put his phone back on the nightstand, and began to sob.

# Chapter Thirty-One

In a cockroach motel outside Bakersfield, Aiden listened to the message over and over. It was after midnight, but the motel was right on the freeway, a truck stop opposite with a diner full of drivers, a gaudy neon sign lighting up the dark. There was noise, a lot of noise, but Aiden found it comforting. He needed that noise, the signs of life, and he soaked it in.

He would miss it.

Listening to Finn's message again, he glanced back into the gloom of the motel room, saw the small figure on the bed, asleep. How easy it would be just to press a pillow over her face, end this all now. Then he could simply walk out into the path of a semi and nothing would matter any more.

Aiden had no idea how she'd gotten him to run with her. He was so crazed with grief, and so horrified that he'd nearly throttled Kenna, that by the time he found himself driving away from San Francisco and from Finn and his life, he could barely think straight.

He gave a choked sob now. There was fucking up, and then there was him. He'd had everything.

So, the temptation to take the easy way out was almost overwhelming.

Almost.

But there was one last thing he could do for Finn. He could give him closure. He could give him justice.

Twenty minutes later, Kenna opened an eye. The room was in darkness and she could feel Aiden's weight as he sat at the bottom of the bed.

That wasn't what woke her though. It was the sirens. She listened intently, waiting, as she had since they'd left for the sirens to pass by.

Except this time, they didn't. They got closer. She sat up and Aiden turned to stare at her. In his eyes, there was a victory and, in that moment, she knew.

Kenna shot up from the bed. "What the fuck did you do? *What the fuck did you do?"*

She darted to the door, but Aiden was too fast for her. He swept her up and threw her over his shoulder as the red and blue lights of the police cruisers filled the room.

Kenna screamed and kicked as Aiden walked out to meet the police, but for the first time in her life, she wasn't in control and she couldn't believe it. *No. No, this didn't end like this, not like this…*

Aiden was relieved when they put them in different police cruisers. Cuffed and behind the grill, he closed his eyes and slumped back against the seat. When he opened them again, the deputy in the passenger seat was looking at him.

"You okay, sir?"

Aiden half-smiled. The dude was more polite than he'd expected the police to be, and he nodded. "Yeah. For the first time in a long time, I think I am."

At twenty-minutes past three in the morning, Detective Pete Krona woke Finn Mason, apologising for the lateness of the hour, then simply said "We've got them."

# Chapter Thirty-Two

*Two years later…*

Finn Mason stood at the door of his restaurant and looked out over the Bay. He was in early, of course. Olly already having left for work, Finn didn't want to hang around the apartment alone.

So, he'd come here, prepared the *mise-en-place*, scrubbed the stainless steel counters and the thick wood butcher's blocks. Hell, he'd even sharpened all the knives, even though they didn't need it.

Better warn Berto and Clyde about that, he grinned to himself, I don't need any lost limbs tonight.

Not tonight.

He breathed in the cool Fall air, the salt scent of the Pacific in his nostrils. Another new beginning. Not the restaurant. *Maison/Mason* had been up and running for a year now and had even won a few minor San Francisco dining awards. Finn was feted, but he still didn't know if that was the ongoing curiosity over what had happened or his food.

"Babe, don't be an idiot," Olly always told him. "People love you for your talent and your food. People will forget the rest of it in time." He kissed Finn softly then grinned. "Also, of course, they want to check out your fine ass."

Finn grinned at the memory, then sighed. He wasn't as convinced that people would forget. He still, sometimes, felt like a sideshow attraction, being stared at, wondered about.

The trial had been long, invasive and shattering. Finn had testified—although he'd tried not to bring Aiden too much into it, it was impossible in the context of events not to—but his ex had smiled and nodded encouragingly at him, understanding why he had to tell the truth.

Aiden looked destroyed. He'd aged, looking exhausted and worn down, but at least Finn knew he was clean. Aiden took his punishment with grace and humility, even making a statement to the court, apologising to Finn directly. He didn't ask for leniency once.

*Not once*, Finn thought now, shaking his head. Aiden was serving a five-year sentence now. With good behaviour he'd be out in three years, but he was never allowed to talk to or attempt to communicate with Finn again.

Ever.

Finn knew he would be lying if he said that hadn't broken his heart. He had hoped, ridiculously he knew, that perhaps he and Aiden could at least be friends.

Olly had looked at him askance when he'd admitted that. "Are you kidding me?"

Finn put his hand on his lover's. "It's not that I want him back. I don't, not even one bit. I'm with you, Olly, I am in this: *us.* But I guess… I guess I miss my friend."

Olly's eyes softened. "I know. But you realize that can't happen now, right? It wouldn't be good for either of you."

"I know." But it still hurt.

What didn't hurt—*at all*—was that Kenna Mitchell was serving a life sentence for attempted murder, arson and a myriad of other crimes. That she was serving it at a mental health facility… well, Finn guessed that was for the best for everyone.

What had come out about her at the trial was horrifying. Her family was old money from Alabama, her father a bigwig in the local Republican family, but they'd cut Kenna off after a series of troubling incidents in her life, beginning with an incident with her much younger cousin. The cousin, a toddler, had almost drowned while in her care. Although no-one could prove it, they suspected Kenna had tried to drown the girl out of jealousy. She hadn't held the kid under water; rather, she had talked her into playing at the water's edge. It was only because a member of the family's staff had been late to work that the kid hadn't died. The staff member reported seeing Kenna watching the flailing child in the water, a smile on her face.

Kenna had been sent to the same school as Lisa Armitage, where she'd bullied the other girl so much that she had switched schools. When Kenna had turned up at the restaurant, Lisa had fallen into a deep depression. They would never know what finally made her jump from the Golden Gate.

Kenna would not admit she started the fire that killed John, and they couldn't find enough evidence to prove it, but Finn knew in his heart that she was responsible. John had been an inconvenience to her, so he had to go.

In the courtroom, Kenna stared at Finn without blinking as he testified against her. Finn kept his cool, didn't get emotional, and simply told his side of the story. The jury had taken less than an hour to find Kenna guilty on all counts.

Finn watched as the verdict was read out and knew Kenna had not expected it. Her self-delusion was so all-encompassing that she never would accept being held to account. She didn't scream and protest as she was led away, just began talking to her guards as if she were telling them that their uniforms were so on point. Finn watched as she disappeared through the door to be taken to her new home and wondered at the psychology of someone who had been given everything in life, but who only found solace in hurting others.

He'd rebuilt his life, a life with Olly. At first, Finn had wondered if it was wise to jump into another serious relationship, but with Olly, nothing ever felt heavy.

Finn had been reluctant to accept money from Aiden's father after the trial, but Glenn Fox would not hear a word about it. "I want to finance your new restaurant, Finn."

"I don't even know that I want another restaurant, Glenn."

Glenn waved his hand. "Don't be ridiculous, Finn, it's in your blood."

And… it *was*. Hannah and Olly were just as enthusiastic and so, after he recovered from his injuries, Finn began to plan. His staff, who had scattered to different places around Castro after the fire, all contacted him when they heard he was reopening, and Finn was brought to tears by their loyalty. Almost all the team came back, except for Jamie who'd gone back to England, but sent his best wishes anyway, chatting to them all via Facetime, and introducing them to his baby daughter, Maisie.

As the restaurant was being fitted, Finn, Olly, Hannah, Berto and Clyde hung out at Olly's place – playing video games, drinking, eating pizza, and trying to figure out a name for the new place.

Hannah, who'd recently relocated to the West Coast to become a managing editor at a new fashion magazine, was the one who'd come up with *Maison/Mason*. "It's quirky, it's fun," she protested when Finn had rolled his eyes.

"It's pretentious."

"Nah," Olly raised his beer bottle, "it's cool. And hey, your mantra for the team is built-in – there is no 'I' in *Mason*, but there is in '*Maison*' so get on with your work, motherfuckers, I'm the boss."

Finn groaned at his bad joke as the others cackled with laughter.

In the end, Finn had come around. "Dude, it's time you tooted your own trumpet," Olly had told him. "Stop pretending you're not an exceptional chef. Believe in yourself."

So, he did, and it felt like a weight lifting off his shoulders. Self-doubt was a killer, he knew that only too well, but in the end, he'd won. He was where he was supposed to be. *Maison/Mason* opened to rave reviews and was booked solid for six months. They'd had to turn away celebrities, for chrissakes.

So, as he gazed out of the door over San Francisco, Finn knew that now, for certain, he was exactly where he wanted to be. He had constructed his life on his own terms. And tonight, he would change it again in a way he never thought he would.

He couldn't wait…

# Chapter Thirty-Three

It was almost closing time, but Finn was still in the kitchen, chopping, mixing, tasting. For once, he didn't care whether his customers had had a good meal or a good night. Tonight, he hadn't made the rounds as he usually would have. He was too busy making sure that the food he was preparing now was the best he'd ever made, that it was executed flawlessly, because there would be no other occasion as important as this one.

Well, maybe one, hopefully...

He felt sick with nervous excitement as Sarah, the hostess, came to tell him that the last customers had left. She rubbed his back and smiled at his nerves. "It's going to be fine, Finn. We're just dressing the dining room now. That smells amazing, by the way."

He thanked her, but didn't look away from the food. He was preparing a recipe that he'd adapted to Olly's particular taste and he didn't want to screw it up. Olly thought he was coming here for his normal midnight meal with Finn—it was a tradition they had started right from *Maison/Mason's* opening. Olly's taste in food ranged from Finn's finest cordon bleu dish to a dirty burger from a sidewalk cart and tonight, Finn was combining both.

He knew Olly would be surprised—usually, after a service, Finn had the energy to make mac-and-cheese with a side salad, but that was it. Not tonight though.

Tonight, he shaved truffles, prepared Wagyu beef, froze little balls of bone marrow with cognac, made a delicate and decadent champagne sabayon. Berto and Clyde julienned vegetables and sautéed rosemary potatoes for the main course and Greg—the pastry chef who Finn had finally persuaded to come cook for him—prepared a lemon tartlet so sharp they all winced.

Greg grinned. "Give it a second."

Sure enough, the flavor mellowed out into a buttery sweetness. Finn grinned at his pastry chef. "You rock."

"Oh, I know."

Finn laughed. His crew, his old friends, plus a couple of new young trainees, were the best he'd ever worked with—minus Lisa and Miko, of course. He'd put their photos up on the huge cork board where he and his staff stuck reviews, recipe ideas and other ephemera.

And… *Aiden.*

*Nope.* He wasn't going to think his ex tonight of all nights. But the good thing was… it no longer hurt as much. In fact, it barely hurt at all any more.

He'd called Glenn Fox, told him what he was going to do tonight, and Glenn had congratulated him. "You deserve to be happy, Finn."

It seemed lately, everyone was telling him that, and for once, Finn would take it. He'd survived… *twice.*

He was happy. His life with Olly was fun, light-hearted, full of new experiences. Olly challenged him every day to try new things and

Finn was learning to reciprocate. He still had the passion for cooking, but he was less stressed over whether *Maison/Mason* was a success. He knew the key now—work hard but play hard too and success would come.

Through Olly, his friend network had grown so much that he realized how insular he had been before, never letting anyone into his and Aiden's life together. Having Hannah in the city brought them closer than ever and Finn tried not to regret the years away from his family. Even his father, Duke, came out to California. He stayed with Hannah, but Finn was amazed that he wanted to spend more time with his son. At first, Finn and Olly kept their relationship away from Duke. But one day, as he and his father were sitting in a coffee house in the city, Finn saw his dad studying him.

"What's up, Dad?"

Duke chuckled softly. "Finn… why don't you hold your boyfriend's hand in front of me? You really think I'm some flyover state hick?"

"No, Dad I just, we just…"

"Son, I *am* a hick, I know that. But… that guy makes you happy. All I could ever wish for you. Anything else is just…" He sighed then then smiled at his son. "Anything else is just bullshit. I'm proud of you, Finn."

Finn thought of that now as he headed upstairs to take a shower and change. *Duke Mason being down with the rainbow—who'da thunk it?*

Finn showered and changed into the simple navy blue suit he'd brought with him for tonight. It wasn't anything fancy—he didn't want Olly, who would still be in his t-shirt and pants from the fire station, to feel out of place—but still, he wanted to be well-dressed for the occasion.

Downstairs, the wait staff had changed too, into fresh uniforms and they were grinning at him, busting his chops as they all waited for Olly to turn up. Berto, Clyde and the others were standing by in the kitchen.

Just after one a.m., Olly knocked on the door and Finn went to answer it. Olly's eyes widened in surprise when he took in Finn's attire. "Fancy boy—what's the occasion?"

Finn pulled Olly's lips to his and kissed him until neither could catch their breath. "*You* are the occasion, Oliver Roberts."

He took Olly's hand and led him into the dining room. Sarah and the others had decorated the empty tables with strings of tiny white lights and candles. The table set up for Finn and Olly was laid out for a silver service meal and Olly, used to a huge plate of pasta, chuckled. "What is this?"

"Please sit, my love. Tonight is all about you."

Olly was still laughing, still bemused but he went along with it and they ate together, being tended to by the staff who played their roles with half-amused seriousness.

The food Finn had prepared was sumptuous and decadent and Olly swooned his way through the truffle-topped Wagyu beef burgers, declaring them the best he'd ever had. Finn grinned—Olly was a burger aficionado and while he could have prepared a myriad of sophisticated dishes for his love, he knew his man.

Olly obviously thought so too. After he swallowed his last mouthful and declared himself replete, he took Finn's hand. "Lover… I appreciate all of this, but what's the occasion?"

Finn smiled, linking his fingers in with Olly's. "Honey, it's been two years. Not that this is our anniversary…well, it is, of sorts. I remember going to the diner and seeing you there and it was on this night when I knew there was more than just a new friend waiting for me. Somehow, even amid all that crap that was happening in my life, there was you and the fact…" He got choked, and Olly chuckled at him.

"Sap."

"Shut up." But Finn was grinning. "I'm trying to be romantic here."

"Sorry."

Finn leaned over the table to kiss him. "What I'm trying to say, Chief Roberts, is that I love you. More than I ever loved anyone. You are my love and my best friend."

Finn's heart was thumping against his ribs as he gazed into Olly's eyes. "I want to be your husband. I never ever thought I'd say that to anyone. But Chief Roberts… would you do me the honor of marrying me?"

Olly laughed out loud, clapping his hands together. His laughter was infectious and Finn began to grin widely. Olly took Finn's face in his big hands. "You're damn right I will, Finn Mason. You're *goddamned* right I will…"

And he crushed his lips against Finn's with a fire that Finn knew would never, ever, go out.

Printed in Great Britain
by Amazon

10420263R00144